enchantments

enchantments

linda ferri

Translated from the Italian by John Casey
with Maria Sanminiatelli

Alfred A. Knopf New York 2005

THIS IS A BORZOI BOOK
PUBLISHED BY ALFRED A. KNOPF

Translation copyright © 2005 by Alfred A. Knopf,
a division of Random House, Inc.

Originally published in Italy as *Incantesimi* by
Giangiacomo Feltrinelli Editore, Milan, in 1997.
Copyright © by Giangiacomo Feltrinelli Editore Milano.

Library of Congress Cataloging-in-Publication Data
Ferri, Linda.
[Incantesima. English]
Enchantments / by Linda Ferri ;
translated from the Italian by John Casey.
p.   cm.
ISBN: 1-4000-4069-8
I. Casey, John. II. Title.
PQ4866.E723 I5313 2004
853'.92—dc22   2003069527

Manufactured in the United States of America
First American Edition

Michel

enchantments

tearing apart

Here comes the cradle covered with white muslin sailing into my room. There's a moment of hesitation, and then the anchor is dropped in the very center so that the little world that was mine now revolves around this newborn sun.

When my sister arrived, there were already three of us—my two brothers, aged seven and nine, and I, who was two. Of the prehistory before she was there I have no mental image; it is before daybreak, everything completely dark.

The next thing I see is my sister in the cradle and a chair next to it on which I'm kneeling, my elbows across the back. I stay there for a bit watching her tiny translucent hands wave in the air. Then I get down and go off to play by myself, waiting for her to grow up.

Not long after that I see an upheaval in our house and a parade of furniture, trunks, and suitcases going down the stairs. Even my little bed is gone, and I'm left alone in the room beside the howling cradle, which is afraid of being alone. There is a frightening emptiness, and the howling cradle resounds in it. I cover my ears and cry.

We are moving to France, to Paris, in Caroline, our fifties Plymouth with gold fins. It's crammed full with our baggage. My father is driving, my older brother beside him. In the backseat there are me, my brother Pietro, and my mother with Clara in her arms.

Our new place was on the ground floor and so dark that my mother dressed my sister and me in bright colors so she could keep an eye on us. Later on, when we'd grown some, she started dressing us in darker colors, but exactly alike.

As we stood in line in the front hall of the nursery school, Clara, expecting that we'd go into the classroom together, kept holding my hand. She cried if Bernadette, the teacher, tried to separate us to do different activities. Bernadette nicknamed her my "little limpet" and arranged the benches in two circles, one for the littler girls and the other for the bigger ones. The circles just kissed each other, and that was where Clara and I sat.

When I turned five, they decided to move me to first grade.

It's evening. As usual at every serious moment my mother is sitting on her bed and I'm standing in front of her, our knees touching, my hands in hers. She explains to me that tomorrow I'm going to a new class but that she and the teacher have worked it out so that at first I'll go to kindergarten as if nothing is different and then at a certain point the first-grade teacher will come to take me to my new class. While my mother is telling me this I feel a wave of fear and excitement, pride and guilt. It's the first secret I have that doesn't include my sister, and when I go back to our room I sit on the floor with my back to her.

The next day as we're standing in line in the front hall, Clara laces her fingers in mine. Mine are limp and damp. We march into class and form our two circles. She starts drawing, peacefully absorbed. On my sheet of paper there appears a house with wavering walls. The first-grade teacher walks in, confers for a moment with Bernadette, and then here it is—she's coming toward me, holding out her hand. I look at that hand, which seems enormous. I look at my sister, still bent over her drawing, then again at the enormous hand. If I take it, it's all over. I close my eyes so it disappears. But then someone brushes my chin, and when I open my eyes I see the teacher smiling at me and I feel important, a sorrowful tragic heroine, so yes, I put my hand in hers, get up, and start walking with my head down. We're almost to the brown door that separates the two classrooms when I hear my sister's screaming that I know so well. But this time it's louder and more terrible, and I, her betrayer, turn around. Bernadette is sitting on one of our little stools, covering it completely with her large body so that it looks as if she's sitting on air. She's holding Clara on her knees, holding her tight around the waist while Clara is thrashing her arms and legs trying to reach me, her mouth wide open in despair. I stand there petrified, but the teacher is already pulling me along, and together we disappear behind the brown door. She leads me to the first row, and still there's that screaming, over and over again, and I collapse on my desk with my head between my arms and sob—long, low sobs during the whole lesson, a grieving faithful echo of the persistent screaming of my sister.

snow white

My first-grade teacher had very white skin and a ribbon in her hair. She called us her "dwarfs" and had us do a ton of fun things—such as pretending that our classroom was a plane, complete with pilot, flight attendant, and in-flight snacks, on its way to faraway lands. After landing, some of us, dressed as Chinese, Africans, or Mexicans, would greet the others, describing our country with the help of books and postcards. All that we did in school was, according to our teacher, "work," and the gentle yet firm tone of her voice kept us in order. I was the youngest in her class, and she brazenly made me her pet. From the very first day she put me in the desk right in front of her and always kept an eye on me, encouraging and praising everything

I did. She told my mother that strictness made me sad.

Sometimes she took me to her home after school. The first thing she would do was to feed me a bowl of soup that sat heavily on my stomach the rest of the afternoon. In that tiny, tidy apartment, with no husband or children around, I discovered the sound of my own footsteps. There were little porcelain animals perched here and there, and two children's busts (a boy and a girl) whose cold, smooth marble cheeks I liked to caress with my fingertips.

Taking me by the hand, the teacher leads me over to say hello to her porcelain animals. "This is Bouncy Bunny, that's Mouse Camembert, and she's Skunky-who-never-listens with her friend Finchy-Pinchy." She tells me that yesterday, with a prodigious jump, Bouncy Bunny landed on Skunky's tail and she got mad as she often does, and let out her noxious cloud, and Mouse Camembert protested to Skunky, who said, "Look who's talking, you stink more than I do," and then Finchy-Pinchy took her friends' side, and that set off such a to-do of pecking and scratching that she had to scold them all, every single one.

"And then what happened?" I ask.

snow white

"Then I put them to bed. You see how well they're behaving. They're sleeping."

"I'd like to see them when they're awake, just once."

"Yes, maybe one day when you come you'll find them playing or working."

At night in bed I imagined the birds chirping, the mice nibbling, and the rabbits hopping in my teacher's house, just like in Snow White's forest. But I never saw them. In her apartment there must have been a spell of melancholy and silence that was broken only when she was alone with her animals.

In the Christmas play she cast me as the Virgin Mary. Mama pinned a silk scarf to my hair, a blue veil that gave my face a rapt and solemn look.

Then my teacher began to get sick, disappearing at first a few days at a time. When she returned she was more thin and pale. Then she disappeared for a long time—an interminable time—and she was replaced by another teacher who shamed me by snatching my notebook from under my nose and showing my classmates how messy my handwriting was.

The last time she came to visit us, she kept her coat on the whole time, and I felt that even

– 9 –

then she was cold. When the time came for her to leave, she said good-bye to my classmates, kissing them on both cheeks. She kissed me only once and held my face between her hands for a long time.

She never came back. Not then, not the next day, not the day after that. But I didn't ask any questions, and in bed at night I kept on imagining her in that house, surrounded by her mischievous scampering animals.

esmeralda

The memory of my teacher faded little by little, a paler and paler ghost that evaporated one day when a doll took over my nighttime dreams. It was one of those women-dolls that you win at carnivals, strangely similar to the girls behind the counters of the target-shooting booths, with a bronze complexion, eyelids with curved eyelashes that open and close over glassy blue eyes, full lips and fingernails painted red, the ruff of her elaborate tulle dress sticking up behind her raven hair.

I had seen her in the home of our housekeeper, Paquita, who was born in Alicante, Spain, and at fifteen had many suitors. One Sunday afternoon she took my sister and me to her parents' home. They acted as concierges in a building in our neighborhood, and the whole family slept in one room, which had a gas ring and a sink. The toilet was in the courtyard.

On one wall was a poster of a bullfight with El Cordobés and a pair of castanets as shiny as chestnuts, and two small mirrors that deformed my face. Seated on the bed, crowning the exotic charm of the place, was the doll. I was dazzled by it, different as it was from the little dolls my sister and I played with.

For all my begging and wheedling, I had to wait a long time before my parents gave me one, and at night in my bed I imagined her lying beside me. I could feel her cool, slightly grainy skin, and I knew her eyes were closed just like mine: a twin, only much more fascinating than I. Finally, one summer day, my father won her for me by shooting a cardboard bear in the mouth at a country fair.

Papa had just bought an ancient Tuscan villa near his native town. It was called Schifanoia—an ugly name and on top of that ridiculous. It means Repel-Boredom, and for a long time I was embarrassed by it. When we went there for the first time, the house was almost entirely empty.

They show me around. Here and there in the large, frescoed halls we see a few dark and imposing pieces of furniture. A smell of mold. Our footsteps echo. And yes, squeaky doors and an inlaid, wooden staircase that creaks with every step. At the top, a door with stained glass in the middle of which gleams a winged dragon.

I'm not at ease in there, and I keep my new doll (not much smaller than I) tight against my hip. The tulle of her pale pink dress scratches my arm and occasionally drags on the ground, which worries me. Then they tell me, "You can go out if you want, but don't go too far. There are Gypsies around." With some hesitation I venture as far as the threshold of one of the glass doors overlooking the park, and I immediately hear a rustling noise in the bushes and see something flash in the green leaves. I step back into the large, vaulted hallway and I call: my mother, my father, my sister. No one answers. I'm afraid I'll get lost if I go looking for them. So I sit in an armchair and arrange the doll on my knees, carefully spreading out her skirt so that I'm hiding behind her. In that deserted and silent room I am pierced by a feeling of unease: it's the villa, it's the Gypsies and the uncertain border dividing us from them, a tribe of nomads camping in a place that doesn't belong to them. And at that moment I find a name for my doll, a magic name, an exorcism that instantly dispels my fear: her name will be Esmeralda, like Gina Lollobrigida in the movie *The Hunchback of Notre Dame,* the Gypsy girl who is as alone as I am now, unhappy and proud, and she will save me from her brothers, furtive shadows in the bushes with an occasional sparkle from an earring or a dagger.

the castrator

Every year we spent three months of our long summer at Schifanoia, so the fear dissolved, reduced to a bit of mystery I carried in my pocket when I made a foray up to the attic or down to the cellar.

My sister and I made friends with the daughters of the sharecroppers who lived in the farmhouse just below the villa, on the other side of an old iron gate that left a fine red dust on our hands. Their names were Mirella and Annarita. They were cousins, about the same ages as us. We played together every day, but not the whole day, since they had chores. We went to get them; they never came to the door of the villa. Early each morning Clara and I rushed down the lane, past the gate, and burst into their house through the door, which was almost always open. We said right off, "So—shall we go?" without saying good morning. We were sure they'd say yes because it seemed to us in the nature of things that children played during the summer. What else should they do? Every once in a while Mirella's long face or Annarita's looking off sideways made us see it wasn't going to happen. "No, we can't. We have to do things." Sometimes Mirella's mother, a vigorous jolly woman, cut it short. "There, chickies, come back tomorrow." That was disappointing—Clara and I would have to play by ourselves, and it felt like wearing a dress that was too tight.

Sometimes we did their chores with them, which ended up making them take a lot more time. Even slopping the pigs became a game for us. Pigs are so mean—when they hear you coming with their feed they throw themselves at the gate of the pen, grunting in a terrifying way. My sister and I would creep closer and closer, and then as soon as the pigs got near us we'd break away with shrieks of laughter and alarm.

When piglets were born, the castrator came. It was a big event. Mirella and Annarita announced it the day before, and I wouldn't have missed it for the world.

With his hat firmly on his head, the castrator sits on a little bench in the farmyard. By his feet he places a small basin into which he pours a purple liquid, a purple so vivid that you see it forever. Then he spreads a handkerchief on the ground, and on it he lays a straight razor that he's taken out of a leather pouch. All of Mirella's and Annarita's families are there. They have a respectful attitude toward the castrator, who is a professional, serious and silent. All of them help, trying to catch the piglets who are running helter-skelter in the pen, flinging themselves from one end to the other, squealing with terror. When they catch one, they put it on the knees of the castrator, who immediately spreads its legs, douses the groin with the purple liquid, picks up the shiny razor, and—zip—a little cut out of which pop two little pink balls which he tosses into a pail without batting an eye.

I watch, hypnotized. What this ritual signifies I don't know, and I don't dare ask. It's a half-closed door to a dangerous room that both attracts me and terrifies me. Behind that door— besides the castrator and besides playing doctor with our friends—there was Saint Maria Goretti, the favorite saint of Mirella and Annarita (my sister and I had picked as our favorite Saint Clara because she was the friend of Saint Francis, who could talk with wolves). Mirella and Annarita took turns telling us their saint's story.

It was a puzzling story because it was never clear
what the saint had refused to do before she was
killed. They liked telling it that way, with shy gig-
gles of embarrassment, and we liked that understanding and not understanding, which made you
want to hear it all over again. We never told
that story. It was the exclusive repertory of Mirella and Annarita, as was the song "Mario, So
Young," which was about a soldier, Mario, who
was in love with a girl, "a swallow of spring."
Mario was sent to the front in Montenegro, and
she betrayed him with a lieutenant. When Mario
came back, he found out and "even though he
lived on poetry," he shot her dead. When the
two cousins sang this—and they chanted it as
intently as a hymn, with a look of bleak fatality—
I got goose bumps and it made my head spin, as
if I were foreseeing the risk I would run by growing up and becoming a woman.

dame dame

In the small garden of our first home in Paris I kept a turtle, Ruga. One morning, when I brought her a leaf of lettuce, I noticed she was gone. So I cried and despaired, but they sent me to school anyway.

That same day at four, on a winter afternoon that was already dark and with the lights on in the living room, the governess who was coming to take care of my sister and me rang our doorbell for the very first time. Even though our avenue was lined not with cherry trees but with horse chestnuts, I nourished the hope of finding myself in front of Mary Poppins, or someone like her in the ways that mattered most, which for me, obviously, were the abilities to tidy up without lifting a finger and to jump into a landscape drawn on a sidewalk and enter a world of merry-go-rounds and cotton candy. Such a person, moreover, would immediately know where Ruga had gone.

As soon as the doorbell rings, Clara and I rush to the door, and never have I been so exasperated by my mother's measured steps. I shout, "Come on, Mama, she's been waiting for ages." Finally, here is my mother opening the door, but I still can't see anyone, because I'm behind her, and all I hear is a voice greeting us from the threshold, and I'm disappointed, the voice doesn't match. Then the governess comes in: the age isn't right, immediately confirming my fears, because Mademoiselle Bernard is already well advanced into that barren zone of gray-white hair and curved backs. The attire also doesn't fit the image, since it's missing two main items: the large handbag and the umbrella. The small hat is there, thankfully: it's not identical, because this is a beret, but at any rate it's there, where it should be, some evidence of deeply desired extravagance, maybe hidden in the large brooch with the end shaped like a Moor's head.

We settle in the living room, and, while talking with Mama, Mademoiselle occasionally smiles at Clara and me, revealing two prodigious, prominent incisors separated by a black hole.

But since Mama always says that neither people's age nor their appearance is important, I
resolutely aim for her soul, searching for some
disembodied affinity between her and Mary Poppins. I am scrutinizing her when Mademoiselle
pulls from her little purse a transparent plastic
box with a gold lid and offers each one of us a red
gumdrop.

That's all: that gesture was enough to
make what hope remained in me collapse. No
matter how you looked at it, Mademoiselle just
wasn't cut from the same cloth as Mary Poppins,
whose magical qualities were blended in my mind
with her brusque and proper manners. So I said
good-bye and went to play in my room, until
Clara came to tell me that it was settled: Mademoiselle would come every day, except for Saturday and Sunday, from three to six.

Dame Dame, as Clara rechristened her,
had been born in 1899, and at some point, a
three-headed Hydra (War, Bankruptcy, Divorce)
had ruined her life. Her father, Henri, had been a
rich textiles manufacturer; her mother, Jeanne,
had been a very beautiful woman, as documented
by a photograph that showed her in a white lace
dress with a tiny umbrella over her chignon,
which was as soft as a nest of feathers.

"You know, girls, it was the *années folles,*" Dame Dame would tell us, and Jeanne and Henri, elegant and in love, made their appearance during afternoon walks in the Bois, at the Longchamp races, at the balls of the Count d'Orgel and the Marquise du Plessy; they went to Deauville and La Baule in summer. War came, and the plant in Poissy went bankrupt; Henri, in despair, began his foolishnesses (Dame Dame never said what, exactly), and Jeanne left home with the three girls. A few years later came the Divorce.

In the beginning, Dame Dame followed my father's uncertain business affairs with an interest tinged with anxiety. And it was enough for Mama or Papa to hint at some difficulty for the Hydra to loom over her yet again. Then Dame Dame, once again, had to face each one of those monstrous heads one by one, so that in her attempts to decapitate them with words she would be compelled to tell her own story from the beginning. It was the Hydra's fault that she had had to look for work very early on without finishing her studies. And later, so as not to leave her mother alone, she had broken off her engagement with André, who had taken her on picnics every Saturday in the Forest of Fontainebleau. For several years she had worked as an assistant to a goldsmith, even at one point designing a ring (which she wore on special occasions) that had received an award at the World's Fair.

Her most ordinary daily gestures were imbued with an aura that brought to mind rare and precious things. For instance, Dame Dame didn't shop in stores but in what she called "maisons." *"Oh, oui, je l'ai acheté dans une très bonne maison, très ancienne, à Filles du Calvaire."* I was fascinated by the exotic names of the Métro stops I had never set foot in, and which gave me the sudden dizziness associated with the mysterious and live metropolis beyond the confines of my bland residential neighborhood, and I was fascinated by those "maisons," which I translated literally and imagined as houses, with beautiful old wooden furniture and ladies who received clients in the living rooms and offered them such exclusive goods that they felt like presents.

Dame Dame was very elegant and cared about how she looked. (I did too, experiencing some satisfaction in noticing her perfect color combinations.) Hats were her forte. She had many: green, pink, purple, with feathers, veils, or flowers, in all styles, and each one left her hair flattened a certain way: shaped like a cloud, a bird wing, or an upside-down bowl. If Dame Dame had taken her hat off and suddenly she thought she heard my father's voice in the corridor, she'd quickly put it back on because he gave her compliments. That was a task he never failed to fulfill, picking on this or that detail that made her look good, maybe with a tinge of irony or a mocking light in his eyes. But Dame Dame was happy anyway.

When she left us at six, she went to work for an old shrew, who on top of it was heavy and an invalid, and she was her companion until the next morning. The old lady was called Madame Rodin, and she was the widow of some sort of philosopher, very famous, and she drove Dame Dame to distraction. She was spiteful and mean, Dame Dame told us. She had driven her mad making her look for one of her little tortoiseshell combs, maybe accusing her of having lost it, until it had turned up under the pillow. "But why don't you get angry?" I would ask Dame Dame, indignant at the old lady's wickedness. She would just shrug her shoulders with an air of superiority. But I was sad to see her leave when it was dark, in winter; I imagined her inside the endless tunnels of the Concorde station, where she changed trains, one hand holding on to her hat,

the other one on her coat, both disarranged by
hot and metallic gushes of wind; then again outside in the cold, climbing up the rue de la Montagne
Sainte-Geneviève, up, up, all the way into the
witch's lair.

In summer, Dame Dame spent a month at
the property that Madame Rodin owned in the
country near Colombey-les-deux-Églises, Charles
de Gaulle's chosen country. And during that
month came the epiphany that rewarded her for
all that year's hard work, her hard fight against
the world's mediocrity, and brought back from a
great distance, from before the War, the Bankruptcy, and the Divorce, an air of grandeur: the
meeting with the General.

De Gaulle had been Rodin's friend, and
every year he made a courtesy visit to the widow.
Dame Dame had the honor of meeting him at the
door and showing him to the living room.

"Bonjour, mon général," she would say to
him, and he would answer, *"Bonjour, Mademoiselle Bernard, je me souviens de vous l'an dernier."*
The scene always played itself this way, and every
year, when she was back from the holiday, Dame
Dame would tell us about it, her face flushed with
pride and emotion, and stupefied that the general
would remember her and her name, moved by his
munificent memory.

la marianne

In France, there was Papa's work, school, and Dame Dame; there were months and months of winter and a few friends of my parents with children who looked sad and pale from too many hours spent in the classroom. As I saw it, France was the country where money was real and good for all seasons, whereas Italian money was fake and good only for summer playtime. There were unequivocal signs of this difference. Italian bills were absurdly large and made our summer wallets look like laundry cupboards overflowing with folded sheets. In such excess I saw proof of their falseness, the way one exaggerates when telling a lie. There were also too many zeros. I preferred the modesty and sincerity of the French, who had eliminated two or three. As for the coins, there were two things that didn't work with the lira: weight and color. Too light the first, gray and devoid of shininess the second, whereas a French coin shone as brightly as a tiny moon in the palm of your hand. But for me, sealing the fate of this monetary duel was the Marianne with her Phrygian cap who adorned the ten-, twenty- and fifty-centime pieces with her young profile and windblown hair, while she appeared full-length on the one-franc coin, as if in the midst of a mad dash, one hand gripping the bag slung across her chest. Where could she be going? And why is she running like that? I wondered. As I could find no answer, the Marianne made me nostalgic for something that I would never know or see, able only to imagine it.

Between the two languages, on the other hand, French was the one that found itself confined to an ephemeral and half-fictitious existence. It appeared on our horizon only at three, with the arrival of Dame Dame, tracing a brief orbit during our games with the "Frenchkids" at the Champs de Mars, only to set abruptly at six when Dame Dame left. We never spoke it at home, and as for school, we attended the Italian one. We wore French easily, like an old outfit with a purpose—gym clothes, a tutu—until we shed it with one casual gesture.

Clara and I had made friends with several

Frenchkids (the two words soon became one in our lexicon). However, Carlo and Pietro couldn't stand Frenchkids. They returned from the park furious and livid with resentment at having been mocked with cries of "*Olé,* torero, Italians-spaghetti-paella."

Once we all got together to record a tape for Grandma Irene, Papa's mother. Carlo declares, into the microphone, "Dear Grandma, Paris is a big and beautiful city. But we don't like Frenchkids, they're conceited and arrogant and they don't even know geography. They mix us up with the Spaniards, and that makes us so angry that the other day we almost got into a fight and for sure the next time they won't get away with it." I'm very struck by how serious Carlo sounds. Usually I don't care what happens to my brothers, but now I think back to Ettore Fieramosca and Barletta's challenge in the school textbook, and so I identify my new role: from now on I will be the sister of the patriots to the rescue, a role that requires a careful balance of apprehension and dignity.

That part, however, soon bored me, because my brothers started getting into fights with Frenchkids too regularly and too eagerly.

For us children, France was Paris, and

when, at the end of summer, we returned by car from Italy, the French countryside looked to us like a vast gray sea that reflected the melancholy that accompanied the end of the holidays. It was the last days of September, and already it rained incessantly on the deserted land that we were crossing. The Frenchkids had started school a while ago, that school that lasted hideously through the afternoon and where there always had to be so much cramming to win some prize or other for honor or excellence. When my parents tried to put me into a French school, I revolted with such violence and determination that they abandoned the idea: Did they really want me to become as pale as the Frenchkids? A sad little grind? Did they really want to bury me alive? No, that's not what they wanted—let's not talk about it anymore. But did they understand me? No, they didn't understand me. France had impressed upon their faces a look of constant stu- pefaction, as if faced with an enduring miracle. My father, who had lived off income from his properties, having found no joy or success in many jobs (as a country lawyer, a salesman of Florentine linen goods in America, a sales rep for a cigarette company in Venezuela), once in France had thrown himself wholeheartedly into a construction venture that made him rich in a few years and gave a heretofore unknown stability to the whole family.

Paris intoxicated them, and they never tired of going out to see it, packing all four children into Caroline: Come on, we're leaving, all the way up to Montmartre to see the city from the top, and at night a whirl around Place de la Concorde, another, and then another and still another.

Papa loved Notre Dame, Mama the Eiffel Tower. I envisioned Notre Dame as a damsel lifting her train with slim arms, and the Eiffel Tower as a playful girl dressed in metal. I imagined that they were friends and, not being able to talk to each other over the din of the metropolis, entrusted their messages to the pigeons who flew tirelessly from one to the other.

My father liked the Louvre, my mother the Orangerie, where the Impressionists were. While visiting the Louvre, I decided that I would be an archaeologist when I grew up, so that I could one day, digging the dead earth, recover the white arms of the Venus de Milo. At the Orangerie, in front of the painting of the cathedral in Rouen at different hours of the day, I decided that I wanted to be an outdoor painter. But one evening my father told me that I was a weather vane, and even a popinjay, changing my mind so often about what I wanted to do when I grew up and shouting it out to the four winds every time. I was upset by that and even felt like telling him that he had changed jobs an awful lot, but I said nothing and from then on tried not to come up with any more ideas, or at least not to go telling him about them. One time, however, I just couldn't hold myself back.

It's Sunday, lunch. We're all sitting at the table in a restaurant called Chez Jeannette. It's an endless bore—it takes them ages to serve us, the conversation languishes, we have nothing to say to each other, it's truly tiresome, and it's just the beginning because, after lunch, our parents have planned to go to the Marché Suisse, an antiques market, and there's nothing Clara and I fear more than a Sunday afternoon (already depressing in itself) spent wandering around stalls of old stuff. Finally we get to dessert and, in front of those bowls, one steaming with a chocolate soufflé and the other dripping with vanilla ice cream, I turn into such a chatterbox that I amaze my whole family. I'm shoveling in a bite of soufflé, a bite of ice cream, bite after bite, and then I take a spoonful of each and swirl them around on my plate until there's a disgusting mishmash, and the whole time I'm talking, I'm saying everything that pops into my head, a bunch of nonsense—that Italy and France are cousins, but I don't know why the French seem like the grandparents of the Italians, grumbling grandparents always a little sad, and the other day when they interviewed me on television and they asked me, "And how about you, young lady, do you prefer Italy or France?" And right there and then I didn't know what to say, because I was thinking of all the beautiful things that are in both countries, but in the end I told them that, at any rate, I wouldn't give up spaghetti not even if I were dead, but I wouldn't give up French sweets either. . . . I'm talking and I'm laughing and I'm eating and I'm talking to fill the emptiness that is in me and between us, and in the end it comes out: "You know, Papa, what I'm going to be when I grow up? The best French-Italian cook of pasta and chocolate soufflé with vanilla ice cream."

My mother laughed, and so did my father, but then he added that I was really completely silly.

the gray czarina

I was almost seven when my father, an
ex–cavalry officer, fell in love with horses again.
And perhaps all I said was "Horses are my
favorite animals. I'd love to know how to ride."
With a magical father like mine, I no sooner
made a wish than it came true in complete galloping reality. By the time I turned seven I had two
Avelignese horses, Usci and Ubi, and two English
Thoroughbreds, Blue Lady and Palmyra Rose.
These horses were "mine," but Papa also had
another, Gonda, a black Friesian mare who
seemed to have come straight from Hell when she
danced her Witches' Sabbath. Every time my
father let her loose in the ring, it was a spectacle.
First she would rear, lashing her tail like a whip,
her long mane flying up to paint the blue sky

black, and when, rejoicing in her power, she beat the earth with her huge fringed hooves and rolled her eyes, she seemed possessed. Then, after she'd calmed down a bit, she would trot along the railing, around and around—one lap, two, three, ten, twenty, fifty. Inexhaustible, she would go by us, shaking her marvelous head, her neck arched high, and my father would say, "Go on, Gonda, go on, you beauty." I said nothing, struck dumb with admiration.

From time to time we hitched her to the driving carriage. That was a long ceremony, what with all the complicated pieces of harness that I was always getting wrong. But then we were off—the creak of the wheels, the crunch of the gravel, and Gonda. If it was winter she steamed and puffed like a locomotive, and at any time she might flick up a pebble that caught you in the face. But above all there was the breeze—not the violent whirlwind coming through an open car window and not the lighter breeze you get on a bicycle that you pay for with sweat—but that movement of air you get in a horse-drawn carriage or on horseback, perfect for humans because it goes so well with thinking.

Usci and Ubi were carriage horses too, but my father made us ride them. That is, my sister and I rode them and their stiff trot jarred our spines. For Clara it was a torture every time, so demonstrably so that she only had to say, "That's enough, Papa, I want to get off," and he was relieved and helped her down. But when I tried to call a halt to the drill, I was promptly rebuffed. "No, you keep going. Make an effort, show some spirit, and you'll do fine. In a few years you'll go to the Olympics, and I'll buy you a horse who'll make Princess Anne die of envy." And I would go on, my legs aching, by now unable to keep a good post.

One day he and I left Paris on a trip, for the first time just the two of us. We were going to Pau, a town in southwest France where there was a family who bred Anglo-Arabs. Rather than being happy, I was fretful, anxious at the thought of all that unaccustomed intimacy with my father, traveling by ourselves day after day.

In the train I began to write. With my fountain pen and a turquoise ink that I adored I wrote down what I saw from the window—field after field like an enormous patchwork quilt and every so often a group of melancholy cows. After a while my father asked if he could read what I was writing. I handed him the notebook without hesitating, but immediately I was sorry. What if he thought it was all foolishness? When he finished, he looked at me seriously. He'd never looked at me like that—a long look of surprise as well as respect. He said, "Good. I like the way you write, I like the idea of the quilt." I was in seventh heaven. But when I started writing again, the muse was silent, and the fields and woods and rivers of drizzly France didn't inspire me any longer.

At Pau we went to the Hôtel de la Poste. Our room was nice, facing the town square where the horse races took place, but it was so small that my massive and portly father couldn't get out of the bathroom if I left my suitcase open.

We went to the races—the couple who bred Anglo-Arabs had innumerable sons who rode in them. The husband was a small, muscular man, a Popeye with a beret, and the wife was a tall stick of a woman, just like Olive Oyl. They addressed each other with the formal *vous,* and I was terribly puzzled that they could have managed to produce so many sons without saying *tu* to each other. With my father I ate snails with garlic and frog's legs.

One day near the end of our stay we chose our horses—three three-year-olds (a stallion, Scapin, and two mares, Urhéane and Ukrainienne) and an Irish Thoroughbred, Ardent Lady. Olive Oyl and her husband gave us a puppy, an Irish setter whom we named Red.

A month or so later, during the summer, the horses (and Red) came from France to Umbria. They were exhausted and nervous. They caracoled out of the truck with a whinnying and stomping that filled me with anguish. The veins stood out on their necks, which were studded with horsefly bites. The men had trouble holding them, and my father told them to let the horses loose in the paddocks, the mares in one, Scapin in the other. They romped around for a quarter hour or more, but when the others settled down, Urhéane was still galloping, with the setter puppy holding on to her tail with his teeth so that he was a red ball flying along twenty centimeters off the ground.

That was how I came to choose her. We grew up together and learned everything together, step by step. Sometimes, for fun, she took the bit in her teeth, carrying me off with her on a rodeo ride the way she did with Red. There was nothing I could do but give her more rein and grip with my legs, sealing in that way the agreement that we were equals, that we would put up with each other's moods without making a fuss.

As far as Urhéane was concerned we were a single thing, and if I had a fear it was that she would count too much on the sure-footedness she had on her own and make a mistake that would bring both of us crashing to the ground.

But I didn't know true fear until later, and that was during the reign of the other mare, the terrible, the gray czarina, Ukrainienne. Even before I got into the saddle my legs would shake. She, who was all quick flesh, could sense my uneasy approach and a current of annoyance would run through her—an annoyance that became intolerable to her once I climbed into the saddle, when I was actually touching her with my plebeian trembling. She couldn't help herself— she had to get me off, soon, right away, now, in whatever way she could. She would rear, time after time after time, with horrifying determination. If I managed to press myself onto her neck, throwing all my weight forward, there she was bucking furiously to make me fly over her head. If I didn't fall right away, she would hurl herself at top speed toward a wall or a railing and then suddenly stop. In a fog I could hear the voice of my father or the riding master telling me to do something, do something—but what? What could I do?

The times when I didn't fall, I still got off in a sea of cold sweat, and in despair. The gray czarina, who a few years later would be—with another rider—the champion of France, was too much for me. But I couldn't bear to admit it. And the day when my mother appeared, shaking with alarm, and yelled loudly and clearly at my father, "Can't you see! You irresponsible maniac, can't you see the child won't ever handle that horse?"—I had my first humiliation.

barbie

Clara and I were the first of our friends to have a Barbie doll. One day a girl joined my class, and her hair was even longer and curlier than mine. I began a conversation by asking her, "Does it hurt you too when someone combs the knots out of your hair?" To impress her I said, without waiting for her answer, "Tomorrow I'm getting mine completely shaved off." She looked so terrified that I liked her immediately.

I found out that she too had a younger sister, and, what was even more exciting, they lived in the same building we'd moved into a few months earlier. I foresaw an endless friendship, total intimacy.

We're in the car. As always my mother has come to pick us up at school. In a rush I tell her about the new girl who's called Anna and who lives in our building, and I point her out with a trembling finger—there she is walking along the sidewalk with her mother and sister. "Mama, can't we take them with us?" I beg feverishly. My mother looks at me intently, weighing the urgency, the seriousness of my plea, and then throws open the door and jumps out of the car and there she is running—running! How my heart is leaping with each stride she takes, a lioness running down her prey for her famished cubs, and I'm thankful, so thankful that my mother is running toward those distant figures on the sidewalk to ask them to come home with us. From then on my mother takes all of us to school and picks us up every day (Anna and Gabriella's father picks us up only after the Saturday half-day). And from then on we play together every afternoon, Mondays at their house and all the other days (except Saturday and Sunday, which are reserved for our family alone) at our house. There was no special reason I could see for this lopsided arrangement, but it suited me because at their house they weren't allowed to play with Barbie dolls.

One day I dared to ask Anna's mother why not.

"Because Barbie has breasts," she replied. And that was that. I didn't dare tell all this to my mother, but that evening I regarded her with suspicion, wondering if it was something to be ashamed of that I had a mother who let me play with a doll with breasts.

Sunday mornings my father would drive Clara and me to the drugstore to buy a new dress for our Barbie dolls. The three of us in the car— Papa at the wheel, one of us in front, maybe both of us. On the radio—sometimes French songs with a mournful accordion, sometimes the races at Longchamp. The quays a gray ribbon running past us, solemn buildings with the windows always shut, cold as mirrors. But I feel cheerful, floating as lightly as our birdlike chatter in the little paradise of our car. "I want Barbie's Christmas dress." "I like Barbie's riding habit."

"And what about Barbie's boyfriend?" my father says. "Doesn't anyone want Ken?"

"No, not Ken," I answer decisively. "We don't like men."

"Not even your old dad?"

"Yes, Papa," I murmur, lowering my head. "Yes." But I'm not telling the whole truth. Because even though I'm very fond of him, I would like him better if he were a woman.

There was one Barbie dress that I adored more than all the others: the Barbie queen's gown. Full-length, billowing, immense, in gold brocade. And then a glittering cape trimmed with ermine. Shoes with gold stiletto heels, a diamond crown, an emerald necklace, and a scepter like a torch holder with a circlet at the top and on it the insignia of the royal family—a big Gothic *B,* blue on a field of yellow. There is a reason that I remember it so well.

One time my parents were invited to a ball at the palace at Versailles.

That evening Clara and I are in our pajamas after our bath. We're sitting in our parents' bedroom on Mama's twin bed. They're getting ready, going in and out of the pink marble bathroom. They're excited, they're talking about this and that, laughing a little. Then Mama takes something out of the closet, some sort of cumbersome bag. She says, "Don't look, children, don't look," and she awkwardly carries whatever it is into the bathroom and closes the door. And I wait endlessly. At last my mother reappears, my mother in the Barbie queen's gown—perhaps not as billowing but full-length, and yes, in gold brocade, and even the shoes are gold. On her face there's a timid smile, but she's very, very happy—I can tell. And my father is smiling and there's a sly gleam in his eyes. He says, "Look under the pillow. . . ." And Mama comes over to the bed where we're sitting and slips her hand under the pillow. And in her hand there is a case made of smooth, smooth green leather with a little press button. And Mama's eyes light up the way a clearing in the woods lights up when the moon suddenly appears, and she asks, "But what's this?" And I know that she knows and doesn't know, knows and doesn't know, and it will be like that, wonderfully like that the whole while she's holding the case in her white fingers, about to press the hard little button. And then, *toc!* Inside there's a necklace of teardrop emeralds. My father picks it up and stands behind Mama. As he gently fastens it around her neck, it closes the circle of my dreams.

indians

My mother was born in America, and she used to tell us bedtime stories about when she lived among the Plains Indians with her grandfather, Sitting Bull. When she got to the end of a story, Clara never failed to say, "Mama, I don't believe your grandfather was Sitting Bull." If Papa was there he'd laugh and say, "What are you talking about? Just look at her big, beautiful Sioux nose." And he'd pinch it and she'd push his hand away, but she'd be laughing too. And she'd add, "Just remember you had to give ten horses to Grandpa Sitting Bull so you could marry me."

She came up with story after story with so many details that even though at the beginning we were just pretending to believe so she wouldn't stop, by the end we found ourselves wondering—what if it's true?

Of course, as we found out the first time she took us to America to meet her family, it wasn't true. To begin with, they were all light-skinned—though there was some hope for an old aunt with a face so wrinkled it looked like cracked shoe leather and an aquiline nose so large it cast a cone of a shadow across her cheek. The only problem was that her name was Rosalinda.

To be sure, Mama's family sometimes spoke odd Italian. With complete assurance they would say they were going to the "supermarchetta" in the "carro." But they weren't Indians—no, they were Abruzzesi, the older ones having emigrated to America at the turn of the century. Great-aunt Angelica and Great-uncle Giacomo (now called Jack) had gotten married by proxy when he was already in America and she was still back in the Abruzzo. Jack told us that he and his brother (my mother's father, who died young) had built the roads of New York State. Jack had gone on to build not only the roads but houses in White Plains, the suburb of New York City where they lived. Perhaps that was why all the houses looked so much alike. When I went for a walk, I got lost. Luckily they weren't all the same color.

Theirs was white, with pink doors and shutters—
it looked exactly like a dollhouse. I'd thought they
might live in a skyscraper. But of all the houses
I'd been in it was my favorite. It wasn't too big,
like Schifanoia, where I had to walk kilometers to
find Mama. And it wasn't too small, like the
apartment in Paris, where your only choices were
the bedroom or the living room—no surprises,
nothing to discover. In Angelica and Jack's house
there were a number of possibilities, but not too
many. If you shouted, somebody would hear you.
The second-floor rooms had dormer windows that
looked like bulging eyes. When I sat close to the
panes, I felt suspended in midair—at the same
level as the branches where squirrels were scurry-
ing and leaping. In the basement there was a
room with wood paneling and a bar with tall
stools. On the walls there were posters of con-
certs and ballets because Angelica and Jack's
daughter was a ballerina and her husband was a
conductor. Next to that room there was a pantry
with a freezer that was always full of broccoli and
ice cream.

At the dinner table Jack would look at me
with his round, transparent eyes and say, "Bella,
eat the broccoli, bella!" And if I didn't eat, Aunt
Angelica would raise her eyes to Heaven, her face

twisted with disappointment, and say, "Oh-ah! You don't like my broccoli, oh-ah!" And then she'd get over it and go on chewing like a cow with a cud, which made my sister and me burst out laughing.

They were very affectionate with Mama, who had lost both her parents when she was young. At meals, Uncle Jack would look at her contemplatively and then blow her kisses, saying, "Oh-ah! Mamie, you are so beautiful!" And then he'd start telling us stories about Mama—how beautiful she had been when she'd met Papa at a boxing match, so beautiful in her big hat and with her velvet eyes, like a Hollywood star. "The Italian" had been bowled over and started a conversation with Jack just so he could meet Mama, who, quite rightly, had played hard to get. But then there was the blizzard of 1947 and New York was one enormous white stalagmite and Mama had accepted Papa's invitation to have tea at the Plaza and when they came back to the house all covered with snow and radiant, Jack had understood that this Italian was going to take his Mamie, was going to take her far away, and Jack was half sad and half happy, happy for Mama because Papa was handsome and smart, but sad because he knew that from then on he would have to live his life without his Mamie.

It was because we lived so far away that Jack and Angelica gave us so many presents, more than to their grandchildren—a mirror with a frame of seashells, two bars of perfumed soap, a porcelain ballerina with a tulle tutu, a plastic bear to put honey in.

A few days after we arrived, Angelica took us to the "supermarchetta," the biggest I'd ever seen. Shelf after shelf of bright-colored boxes. Angelica, Clara, and I each took a cart and loaded them as if we were shopping for a family of giants. Broccoli and ice cream, of course, but also Sara Lee brownies (which we'd already tried) and Oreos, black outside, white inside, a dramatic contrast of chocolate and cream that seduced us as soon as we saw them. And finally popcorn in its own little pan sealed in tinfoil. You put it on the stove, and then there was a mysterious hissing and then the foil puffed up into a wonderful silver ball. You punctured it with a knife, and there before your eyes was the popcorn, as fluffy as a pile of cotton balls.

On weekends my mother's cousins came to visit. They were more like her sisters since they'd all grown up together. I liked Laura because when I talked with her I didn't feel backed into a corner the way I did with other grown-ups. Talking with Laura was like walking around in a big, airy room. I could ask her anything. Whereas Mama became impatient when she had to explain things, Laura always made an effort to find a reasonable answer. Alba, my mother's other cousin, who was Angelica and Jack's daughter, fascinated me because she'd been a great ballerina. I tried to imitate the way she walked with her feet resolutely turned out.

Laura had a daughter my age, Kate, who was the most beautiful girl I'd ever seen. In the photos they took of us she's always smiling while Clara and I look like sullen old ladies. One time, as a joke, Kate put the clasp she used on her dog, Piccola, in her hair. When she laughed and turned toward me, I felt pierced by her splendor.

Alba had two children, a boy and a girl. They all thought the boy was a genius. He had a complete collection of *Life* magazines and a chemistry set. One time his sister broke a test tube, and he threw himself on the ground screaming. Clara and I had a fit of hysterical laughter, which made it all the worse—the more we laughed, the more furiously Tommy beat his fists on the floor. His sister, Norma, dressed like Sports Barbie, and her bedroom was just like Barbie's, white and fuchsia, with upholstered night tables and lace around the bed and windows.

With these cousins we spoke some English and some Italian but more Italian because they were intent on learning it. My mother said, "They're smarter than you, they're thinking ahead. I have four provincial children who are embarrassed to speak English. But you'll be sorry one day." It was true that I was embarrassed to speak English. When I was on vacation in Italy I was embarrassed when it came out that I knew French. It would be worse when they found out I also spoke English. For some reason, wherever I went I wasn't like most people. In France, they knew I was Italian. In Italy, they knew I lived in France and had an American mother. In America, they knew I came from one old country or other, whereas here everything was brand-new. My American cousins already knew at the age of seven what university they would go to. I had the confused and unpleasant feeling that nothing in me was there for a reason, nothing had any purpose. In their lives everything made sense and was bound to flourish. So being with them made me feel old, old and worn out and with nothing ahead of me.

judas

Yes, my parents quarreled.

Paris, an evening like any other, all of us at dinner, my father at the head of the table. We're talking about school—my brothers' report cards or tests. Mama complains about them a bit, Papa raises his voice—in my brothers' world the usual routine of failings and reprimands. It goes on like this for a while, until a different note in my father's voice gets my attention, that unequivocal freezing of his voice, as if it has suddenly crossed a cold current, and I know that the chain has snapped: he's not barking anymore, he's ready to bite. This time it's Pietro, the younger of the two, who has perhaps looked up with a grin and is now getting up from the table to retreat to a safer place. He still hasn't left the dining room when my father's shoe hits him in the head, drawing blood from his temple. My mother jumps to her feet and rushes to him. And there she is lifting her bloody hand like a battle standard while a roar rises up through her—from what deep dark cave of resentment and blame I don't know, but I'm terrified. I don't recognize her.

There's a shouting match between my parents, with words like claws that tear my heart to pieces. Words such as *separation* and *divorce.*

Then, when my father leaves the room, a long silence knots our throats until my mother says to me, "Go to your father, don't let him be by himself." Of course I go, because after a family quarrel it's almost always up to me to go from one to the other with the same message: "Come on, don't be hurt, we're like the fingers of a hand, inseparable." But there's a hesitation in my steps, and the words that I'm preparing for my father are caught in my throat like the long silence at the table.

It's dark in their bedroom. Papa is in the bathroom, the door open. He's washing his face, getting ready to go out. But the worst moments aren't over. He's still breathing hard, and his face is twisted, his nose and mouth out of place. He picks up a towel, and that face disappears in its whiteness. I'm standing there beside the sink, I don't know what to do, and I still have that knot in my throat but now it's worse, it's my heart throbbing with embarrassment and sorrow. I see my hand reach out toward him. It touches his arm, and at last a sound slips out—"Papa . . ." His voice breaks through the whiteness: "Go away, Judas. I know you're on their side." I step back as if slapped, but I'm relieved in a way, because I deserved it. Yes, I'm like that Judas person—some sort of woman famous for having preferred her mother to her father.

witchcraft

My father tilts his head back, his eyes bug open, and he makes a thread of saliva come out of a hole under his chin—a wound from his days as a partisan. We call it "mooky-worm." My father knows when it's about to thunder, he knows the spell to attract fireflies into the palm of your hand. My father has a friend who is a witch and who can—if we turn off all the lights in our bedroom—make it rain candies. My father can transform himself into a fire-breathing dragon, into a hypnotizing snake, into a child-eating ogre.

Sometimes I'm embarrassed by him in front of my friends because he calls them "his little old ladies." He always exaggerates. When we invite my friends to a restaurant, he forces them to eat snails or, at the Chinese place, snake soup.

And I'm embarrassed by him when he swears that as soon as Clara and I have suitors he's going to kick them head over heels down the stairs. And I'm embarrassed when he sends our dressed-like-an-admiral doorman to pick us up at school.

Sometimes he surprises me, taking me to eat ice cream at the Hilton at eleven at night or to a late movie in the middle of the week. When I'm the one to ask him to take us out he surprises me: "Yes, tonight we're going to the Teatro Bianchini with blankets and cushions." Then I might sit on his knees and lay my head on the curve of his stomach. And there, sucking a cube of sugar dipped in cognac, I can feel the very center of his breathing.

Sometimes I adore him. I throw my arms around his neck, and I smother his broad face with kisses: the chin, the eyes, the nose, the cheeks rough as sandpaper. When he returns from a trip I adore him, I throw my arms around his neck, and I see myself in his exuberance, I see myself in his bright, happy eyes. One time he and Mama don't tell us they're coming back from their trip to South America and the doorman/admiral makes us go round and round before letting us in, and when we go into the apartment it seems as deserted as ever. But in the bedroom, on each of our beds, is a mountain of presents, yes, truly a mountain, and sometimes there's a landslide and part of it falls to the ground (a sombrero, an Inca mask, a colored cymbal), and Clara and I know that they're back and we start looking for them frantically, but they're not in their room, so we open the bathroom door and there they are, radiant, with Papa trying to hide behind Mama, even though he's too big. Because it's not enough for him, he wants more games, more magic, more marvels, until something moves between his feet, a poodle puppy, with a red ribbon around its neck.

Sometimes my father scares me.

I have locked myself in the bathroom, and now he's at the door. I've done something bad, and he's at the door. He says, "Open." I think of his thick, hard hands, and I don't open. But I sense something more terrible than those hands, I don't know what it is, but it won't go away if I stay behind that closed door. I hesitate. I hesitate so much with my fingers on the key that my legs shake. My father scares me even though he has hit me only once.

We're passing the border at Mont Blanc. It's summer, it's very hot, and we're stuck in a long line of cars. It's not moving at all. They all go to get something to drink. "Come on," they say, and I answer that I'm tired and would rather stay there. The truth is, I want to pretend I'm driving. I like to turn the steering wheel, make long big swoops as if I'm flying around the earth. But the wheel is burning hot and I give up. I look out the window, but there's nothing interesting to look at, only a man in his undershirt picking his nose leaning against the door of the car next to ours, and after a while I'm bored. I regret not having gone to the café with the others. Then I remember the penny that Papa gave me. I pet my pocket and pull it out. It's brand-new, blazing red. I look at the profile of the murdered president and think that I wouldn't want to be president of a country like America where there are so many people and, of course, some crazy person who might decide to shoot you. I turn the penny around, but there's little to see on that side, only some kind of a monument with pillars. So I start playing around with the coin, trying to make it roll from one finger to the next, but I'm not very good and the coin falls on the floor. I bend over to pick it up, and as I'm getting up I notice the ignition. The hole is about the same size as the penny. I wonder if the penny fits. Yes, it's perfect. Exactly the right size, so I stick the coin in several times. At first just a little bit, then more and more, until it's half, more than half, until I only have a sliver between my fingers. Suddenly the penny disappears into the hole. I don't worry right away. I try to get it using a hairpin that I find in the glove compartment. But I only make things worse; all I can see now is a thin red line deep inside the hole.

I start sweating. I'm in a panic. I'm so terrified I can't think what to do. So I curl up on the floor in front of the passenger seat and weep.

"What are you doing down there?" my mother asks when they get back. "Come on, get out of there, we're going to start moving soon." She opens the car door, and I slide out. I'm so paralyzed by terror I don't move easily. I climb into the back and cling to my sister, who tells me to go away, it's too hot.

My father gets into the car and sits at the wheel. He is talking while holding on to the keys, occasionally throwing them in the air, and my heart goes up and down with those keys until he says, "At last, we're moving" and tries to stick the key into the opening. But the key won't go in and my father says, "What the hell is this?" People behind us start honking their horns, and

Papa swears and keeps trying, again and again. Suddenly he turns his head and looks at me.

I confess instantly, and as soon as he starts hitting me I feel better, much, much better, because, yes, it hurts, but the fear, the fear of my father, which isn't the same as the fear of his hitting me—that is the more terrible thing.

the bukowski brothers

My sister's face is the first thing I see each morning and the last thing I see at night—and her eyes, big and round as pebbles in a stream, shining even in the dark.

For the composition "My Sister" that the teacher assigned me over the Easter holidays, I manage to write only a few lines: that Clara calls anything she really likes "fantasmagoric" and that since she was a little girl she's been attracted by the moon and by astronauts and that when she's happy she starts bouncing on her bed yelling over and over, "Fantasmagoric! Yuri, Gagarin, Yuri!" I can't write anything more than that, even if I know everything about her, since we're one single being.

With my brothers it's exactly the other

way around. I don't know them, but because of the distance between us, I can describe them very well. I see them as members of a small tribe of savages occupying a territory that borders ours but is quite distinct. I witness their daily rituals, I see them kneeling on chairs for hours, absorbed in newspapers spread out on the dinner table; or patiently lining up row after row of toy soldiers only to mow them down with a single backhand swipe and warlike sound effects. I also see them bouncing and squirming on the bed, alternately laughing and howling like madmen as Papa whips them with the belt of his trousers.

It also happens that we're the objects of their raids. We find our dolls hanged on the drawstrings of the curtains or dangling on the branches of the plane trees out by the street. Until now we've put up with all of it, with their stupid jokes, like pulling away the chair when we're about to sit down at the dinner table, and even the tickling torture when one of them holds our arms down on the bed while the other one runs his fingers up and down our whole body. . . . But the execution of our dolls, no, that we really can't put up with. And when we discover this outrage, this cruelty, this profanation, we fill the house with our screams.

I scream more than Clara, louder and louder, a storm of tears and rage, and I start pulling my hair out. That frightens my sister, who stops crying. She comes over to me, leans her head on my shoulder, and says, "Come on, don't get so upset," and then I feel even worse because now I'm the only one who's going to make things right, and I throw myself on the ground and tighten my whole body until it's rigid and my face turns purple. I'm gathering all the strength I have in me, and I'm about to go into convulsions, when Papa and Mama rush in and shake me, saying sternly, "That's enough, that's enough now. Get up. Pull yourself together."

I emerge from this fit exhausted and pained, as if I'd fallen in a deep well. For weeks on end I don't deign to look at my brothers, not a single glance . . . until they lure me once again with the circus game.

Carlo announces at the top of his voice, "Ladies and gentlemen! Boys and girls! Kind public! This evening we have the great honor and pleasure of presenting to you a sensational act! Straight from Russia, the fantastic, the marvelous, the incredible Bukowski Brothers!" and Clara, Pietro, and I burst into the room trumpeting the fanfare.

It's eleven at night. Papa and Mama have gone out, confidently thinking that we're tucked in bed. Not tonight—tonight we're putting on the Bukowski Circus. We'll do somersaults, tumbling, balancing acts. I, under the name of Galina, will succeed in standing (without using my hands) on the bent knees of Ivan-Pietro. Next to us Boris-Carlo will lift Olga-Clara into the air holding her by the calves—a prodigy of strength and talent. Ladies and gentlemen, marvel at the Bukowski Brothers! And for a finale the two boys will perform their celebrated Kiss the Wall of Death. They will climb onto the foot of the bed and let themselves fall stretched out full-length toward the headboard, each time starting a centimeter closer to it, an act that frequently ends up leaving frightening bumps on the foreheads of Ivan and Boris.

Clara and I are having a wonderful time, we're thrilled now that the brothers' strength, energy, and daring—so often opposed to us—are on our side, almost at our service. It's encouraging us, spurring on the daring that's in us, a fragile bud that has never blossomed. But now everything is possible, and Clara and I are imagining new acts, more and more reckless, because Galina and Olga can levitate, walk on burning coals, or do a tightrope act on the balcony railing, they can positively fly. Then the great moment will arrive and Boris and Ivan will throw wickedly pointed daggers at the sisters backed against the tapestry in the living room with its hundred Moorish domes, and Galina and Olga will stand there—imperturbable, without a tremor, without the slightest movement of their lips or eyebrows, putting themselves into their brothers' hands with the natural faith that the strong have in the strong.

Pervor

Mama, who is a Lady of Charity for the Catholic Mission, takes me with her to see an Italian family who live in Nanterre, in the shantytown. We walk along unpaved alleys and one of my shoes gets stuck in the mud, and when I try to pull it free my foot comes out of the shoe and I balance for a second on one leg but then fall over and there I am with my kneesock in the muck halfway up my calf. My mother gets mad. Moving brusquely and grumbling the whole time, she hangs the shopping bag full of food on a fence post, pulls the shoe loose, takes off my sock, turns it inside out, puts it in her overcoat pocket, and puts the shoe back on my bare foot. "There," she says, "let's go," and she doesn't say anything until we reach a shack with a sheet-metal roof.

"It's here," she says, and knocks on the door, which isn't much bigger than the front of a cupboard. A girl a little smaller than me opens the door. She has on a red wool dress that I recognize—it's mine, though by now it's too short even for my sister. Six or seven other children are swarming in the room. From the back there comes a voice from a bed. The bed is pushed against a wall covered with cardboard. "Come in, Signora. Please sit down. Excuse me. I don't feel very well today."

My mother puts the shopping bag in a corner and goes to the bed, but I don't dare follow her. I stay in the middle of the room with all those children milling around. They laugh, chase one another, joke in an exaggerated way without saying a word to me, but they keep looking at me sideways as if to see if I'm enjoying the show. I, on the other hand, want to hear what my mother and the woman in the bed are saying to each other, and I prick up my ears across the hubbub. I manage to make out my mother saying, "precautions," though I don't really know what it means. The lady says, "My husband doesn't . . ."

Then my mother calls me over to introduce me to the lady, who holds out a hand that is callused but weak, so so weak, and even her smile has no strength, and suddenly I feel a pity I've never felt for a human being, I've felt it only in the countryside for a sick dog or a swallow with a broken wing.

After a while we leave. By now it's dark. I feel the cold mud on my ankle, but I don't say anything. Instead I ask my mother what "precautions" means.

"It means something one does to avoid something happening that's dangerous or unpleasant."

I press a little. "And that lady has made a precaution?"

"No. That lady has not taken precautions," she says, correcting me. She's in a bad mood, so I let it drop.

The next day we have a religion lesson. A priest, Father Tonioli, a recent addition to my school, reads us the Gospel. He thunders from the lectern: " 'Verily, verily I say unto you: it is easier for a camel to pass through the eye of a needle than for a rich man to enter the Kingdom of God.' "

I'm tremendously impressed, and day after day I hear in my head that sentence of Jesus, and I see the lady in the bed. At home we never talk about religion or anything along those lines, so I go to the priest. But I can't put together a proper question, I can only tell him about the lady, and then I repeat the sentence about the camel. The priest has a straightforward answer: he explains to me briefly and understandably that the world is, alas, divided into rich and poor and that Jesus definitely prefers the poor.

At home I ask my father if we're rich or poor. "We're poorer than some people and richer than others," he replies, leaving me straddling that troublesome dividing line. At any rate, I grasp that we're richer than a great many people, and the next day I go back to Father Tonioli with the question "How can Jesus love me if I'm richer than so many other people?" Father Tonioli explains to me that Jesus loves everyone but that he will love me even more if I love the poor, if I will give up my own gratification and defend them and help them, day after day, without boasting about it.

From then on I always ask my mother to let me go with her to visit the family in the shantytown. I begin a sort of friendship with the girl who wears my red dress. Some months later another little brother is born, and although she's the one who usually gives him his bottle, she sometimes lets me do it.

I go to Mass every Sunday, by myself, since

my parents apparently aren't interested, nor are my brothers. Sometimes Clara comes with me, but she does it only to be with me. At church, after the Our Father, as the Mass is getting near the end, I look up at the vaulted ceiling, where a multitude of saints flies around among fluffy white clouds like meringues. A wave of happiness and gratitude comes over me at the thought of the meringues with whipped cream that are waiting for me at home at the end of Sunday dinner. But then I'm suddenly alarmed: with that sort of selfish joy I won't set foot in the Kingdom of God. I sadly resolve to save my meringues for my friend in the shantytown.

One day my father comes home with a basket full of oysters, smoked salmon, and a jar of caviar. I don't know why, but he's in a wonderfully contented mood. He says, "Tonight we're celebrating."

"Why?" I ask him.

"Because we're a nice family, because we're all well. Because Paris is a marvelous city."

For some time now my father's indifference to the poor, the love of Jesus, and the Kingdom of God has been offending me. So I confront him, but in a roundabout way.

"You know, I'm lucky, because I don't like

oysters or salmon or caviar, or any of those expensive things."

"Ah, is that right?"

"Yes. And the money that I don't spend buying them I'll give to the poor people."

"That's nice that you're concerned with the poor," he says, but he's distracted, intent as he is on opening an oyster with a knife, and I can't bear it, his selfish greedy happiness is grating on my nerves.

So I come up to him and with my mouth close to his ear, pronouncing each word clearly, I say, "It is easier for a camel to pass through the eye of a needle than for a rich man to enter the Kingdom of God." The knife slips in his hand, and he nearly cuts himself. He's furious. He stares at me with a terrifying look, and then he yells, "Get out of here! Christ Almighty—get out of here, you pious little prig!"

And I burst into tears and go shut myself in my room.

lucifer

Dame Dame always told us, "When you're playing in the Champ de Mars, watch out for men roaming around in the bushes. Most of all for the ones with raincoats." But when I asked her what was particularly dangerous about men in raincoats, she replied even more enigmatically, "Under their raincoats they may be hiding a nasty surprise." No, I definitely didn't understand. On the other hand, what she didn't understand was how one day I had managed to get my legs in such a state, bleeding from long thin red welts. "But how did you do that? Tell me how you did that," she scolded me. "It looks as if you're wearing fishnet stockings."

"I scratched them on some bushes playing hide-and-seek with Aude," I lied, because I certainly couldn't tell her that these were wounds from a glorious and holy war.

It had begun some days earlier.

In the bushes I am looking for bad boys, in particular a boy with thick eyebrows curling up on his high pale forehead, with two gray eyes like ice, beautiful as Lucifer and equally proud and wicked. The boys are in a gang that attacks weak defenseless little girls. They hide in the bushes, and as soon as they see a girl, alone or with a friend, they jump out and, armed with long switches, whip the girls' legs, yelling, "Death to the vile sex!" They've come after me twice, without being able to hit me because I can run fast, certainly faster than they. But even if I've escaped, now I say that's enough—justice must be done, and I am the one to do it.

I pull up a nice thin sapling by the pond and trim it well, pulling off the leaves and twigs until it shines in my hand, smooth and slick, naked as the sword of an archangel. I carefully approach the corner of the Champ de Mars where the gang usually hangs out. I hide behind a plane tree, and from there I see them in a clearing, sitting on a bench, conspiring. I calculate—from my hiding place to the bench is about thirty meters. Yes, I can do it. And then I leap out—I

have to do it right away or I won't do it at all—I
leap out and in a flash I fall on them, making my
switch hiss on the thin calves of the astonished
Lucifer. Then I take to my heels, a mad dash, my
heart in my throat, until I reach safe territory,
until I reach Dame Dame on her bench and let
myself fall across her knees, exhausted. When
she asks me with alarm, "What is it? What's happened? Say something!" I mumble, "Nothing,
nothing. I thought there was a rabid dog chas-
ing me." And I stay there on her knees, gasping
for breath but proud, with a pride that fills me
completely—even if it puzzles me because I don't
know (and don't want to know) if what is making me so proud is the punishing of the wicked,
the rendering of justice, the crusade on behalf of
the weak, or is it having done all this in front
of the beautiful Lucifer—against him and yet
for him.

Afterward, naturally, I wait for their revenge, I wait for it with fear and trepidation. But
since day after day it doesn't come, in the end I
go looking for it. Without my switch I penetrate
the enemy lines.

And once I'm there, once they're on me
with their switches and Lucifer is whipping my
legs methodically and coldly, I don't make any

attempt to run away but give myself up in total surrender.

Because to those afternoons without the wicked boys prowling about, without a perversely beautiful Devil with whom to contend in a fight to the finish between Good and Evil—to those insipid afternoons I surely prefer their whippings.

heart throbs

My first men were waiters and gas station attendants, bakers and bus conductors. Fleeting encounters without entanglements. Enough distance between us so that I could train myself safely in the gymnasium of seduction. They attracted me, but that wasn't the point. The important thing was that I attracted them. I used them unscrupulously, as mirrors.

On the bus, the test of the gaze: to manage to keep looking into his eyes while he punches my ticket. At the restaurant, my hand resting lightly on the table, tilted a bit to hide the childish roundness so that when he comes back with the macédoine he discovers it—a white butterfly with trembling wings. On my way to the corner where there's a gas station I walk any old way, but when I get there—a few meters before—I slow down.

Back straight, stomach in, eyes straight ahead. Above all not looking at him but checking to see if he's there without looking (I already know how to do that quite well). Then feeling his look like a hot beam. Putting an indolent sway into my walk.

It was only later that I tried riskier enterprises. A fifth-grade classmate—Giovanni Tini— chubby, shorter than I, with thick-lensed glasses. One day I found in my notebook a paper boat with a figurehead in the shape of a red heart, on which I read "G loves M as Romeo loved his Juliet." There was another boy in my class whose name began with G, Gianluca, but it couldn't be him, he was too engrossed in his revolutionary reclassification of beetles. It had to be Giovanni.

At home I asked Mama who Romeo and Juliet were.

"Two young lovers. Their families were enemies and they didn't want the lovers to marry, so Romeo and Juliet could only be together in death."

"Have you and Papa quarreled with Giovanni Tini's parents?"

"No. Why?"

"Nothing, I was just asking."

I went back to my room. I felt confused, and that story about dying so they could live together worried me.

So I temporized, flirting with Giovanni just enough to enjoy his courtship. My notebook was the port where the white packet boats of his love dropped anchor. "You are my sweet Juliet." "How beautiful and fair you were yesterday with your hair in long braids like Juliet's." "You have dark eyes like Juliet's."

But his pomposity, and the way I had to bend down when I spoke with him as short as he was, and the pathetic way he groped around when our classmates knocked his glasses off his nose—it didn't take long for all this to become tiresome. And one Saturday afternoon at a party, without thinking about it beforehand, I found myself ferociously destroying his adoration.

I tore up and down the hallway like a rocket and ended up throwing myself across a divan screaming all the dirty words I knew. And the more incredulous and shocked he became, the more I taunted him, sticking this desanctifying dagger in up to the hilt. Finally a look of contempt came over his face. Only when I left, exhausted, did I begin to feel ashamed. The next Monday, after recess, I found a ship in my notebook made of black paper. The heart-shaped figurehead had been replaced by a white cross on which was written, "Juliet is dead. She fell off the balcony like a tomboy."

For a while I felt bad about ending it—I was that vain—but I got over it when a new boy arrived: Lorenzo, from London. A sweater with holes in it, torn jeans with bell-bottoms, a purple velour pullover with the slogan "Make love, not war" sewed on the sleeve. All of it from Carnaby Street. A face with a constant play of feelings, cherry-red lips, and lively tender eyes. Infinitely more up-to-date than we were, he talked about taboos, the bourgeoisie, flower children, and rock groups I'd never heard of. One morning the teacher called on him to recite a poem we'd had to memorize.

Standing beside the lectern, Lorenzo began. At first his eyes were on the teacher. "We buried on this battlefield our youngest and our strongest. His only badge of valor the wounds upon his chest." Then, as he became more impassioned, he turned toward the class as if moved by a current: "Machine-gun fire has mowed him down like wheat before a scythe. . . ." At last, his eyes filled with tears, he clenched his fists and held them out toward me—straight toward me. I was thrilled, trembling, captivated as he recited the last prayerful stanza: "And now the farmboy soldier's soul is in Thy hands, O Lord. Grant his comrades' prayer for him—a hero's paradise!"

From that moment I felt an awakening in

my heart, which fluttered like a caught bird. I would run breathlessly up the stairs at school to catch a glimpse of him in the main room standing in line for class. When he arrived late, I agonized. When he was absent, I felt abandoned by the world.

Then, one evening, I found out that he loved me too.

At eight the phone rings. My mother answers. "It's for you," she says. "It's Lorenzo." I take the phone. My hand is trembling. I say, "Hello?"

"Hi, it's Lorenzo. I wanted to ask you—tomorrow, for the arithmetic work in class, should I bring graph paper or lined?"

Afterward it dawns on me. What sort of question is that? It's an excuse. I shout, "It's just an excuse!" and run into my room. It's one of the May evenings in Paris when the day doesn't really want to die and the twilight is glowing and still. I'm sitting on my bed, near the window. I look outside, and in my ecstasy, which I am holding the way the day is holding the light, I see nothing, I hear nothing, I don't exist anymore, I'm not these arms, these legs, this head—all of me is in the frantic beating of my tiny chest.

brigitte bardot

Some Sunday mornings Clara and I would get up before our parents. As quiet as mice, we'd go to the kitchen to make orange juice for them (the squeezer, unfortunately, made an infernal racket) and get the coffee machine ready. Then we'd run back to our room—still quietly, because waking them up would spoil everything. Remembering to take the key, fly down the stairs and gallop all the way to the bakery on Rue de Laos to buy chocolate rolls for Papa and croissants for Mama. The last stop was at the florist to get red carnations for Mama. That was her favorite flower—she said it had that faint faint odor of a newborn baby—and luckily they cost the least, one franc each, so we could give her a bunch of five and sometimes ten. Once we were back at the

house we made as much noise as we could—
everything was ready and we couldn't wait to see
their look of surprise and pleasure. (After a few
times, of course, they weren't so surprised, but I
still delighted in the role of the perfect daughter.)

Some Sunday mornings my father was the
last one up. About eleven.

In his baggy boxers and undershirt he
makes his way to the living room and turns on the
record player. He gives a huge yawn and starts
leafing through records, humming a tune. Suddenly he stops, raises his eyebrows (his eyes are a
little bit red, a little bit white, like a monster's),
and then turns toward me and produces an
angelic smile. At last he chooses a record—Fred
Buscaglione—which he adores because it makes
him remember I don't know what kind of good
times. He puts it on and turns up the volume. He
starts to dance, with spins and hops that are
exaggerated and awkward. One of us always
says, "Papa, you look like a gorilla." He expects
this, and it does nothing but make him wilder.
And then there he is taking my hand so I'll dance
with him, and I'm blushing and laughing. I go
along for a few steps. At the same time I take in
the words of the song—"I saw you, I followed
you, I stopped you, I kissed you, you were so

young, so young . . ." and I happen to notice the record jacket on which there's a photo of Buscaglione with a mustache and a croupier's eyeshade. He looks dangerously like my father when he was young, when he too was a confirmed gambler, and it occurs to me that this is a part of his life that someone should be paying attention to. Every time my father plays a Buscaglione song I listen very carefully to the words, and I get an overwhelming impression of a murky red world where it's always nighttime, and there's kissing and fighting and a lot of platinum blondes who don't look anything like my mother.

It makes me nervous and worried, and I begin to keep an eye on my father, all the more attentively since my mother seems to be unpardonably unaware.

One evening he comes home from a business trip, and he tells us that at the airport in Nice he ran into Brigitte Bardot. He has a sly look, and as he's talking he keeps glancing at my mother, as if he's thrown down a gauntlet. She's not really paying attention, isn't the least bit interested in picking it up. Now Papa is saying that the actress smiled at him, and he imitates the way she walked, her head turned toward him, trailing a smile behind her like a long net. Then he opens his suitcase and takes out two pairs of sunglasses for my sister and me. They're huge, with mod frames covered with fluorescent checks. My father says that Brigitte Bardot had glasses just like these. When he holds them out to me I throw them into the air, and I shout that they disgust me and Brigitte Bardot disgusts me, and once again I burst into tears and go shut myself in my room.

perfidy

For some time now I've been suffering from stomachaches, cramps that keep me in bed with my arms wrapped around my body. Mama takes me to the doctor and that is how I come to take medicine for the first time, brown pills, sweet on the outside and tasting like flour inside.

Mama tells me that I mustn't worry so much about school, and I say, yes, I'll stop worrying. But it's not school—it's Teresa who's giving me stomachaches.

She came into class one day with her darting eyes. The school year had already begun, and the principal brought her in to introduce her to the teacher and her new schoolmates. While the principal was speaking, Teresa's eyes never stopped moving from one face to another. I thought of the pellets of mercury that run out of a broken thermometer, and I didn't notice anything else about her, just those restless eyes. After yet another frantic tour of the room, her eyes suddenly stopped at my face, examining my cheeks, mouth, and nose and at last fastening on my eyes and not letting go.

By the third day we were inseparable.

We saw each other after school almost every day, usually at her house since Teresa was an only child and her parents were always out. That way there was no one to distract us when we wrote our novel about a queen of heaven named Aurora Borealis, or to spy on us when we planned our crimes. We were going to steal four rings, three hatpins, and a rhinestone necklace from a department store. It was a robbery that we prepared meticulously, but right in the middle of it she bolted, leaving me standing in front of the display case with the open shopping bag in my hands. Of course I ran too, dropping the empty bag. I didn't speak to her for two weeks.

We were both good at schoolwork. And we made a pretty picture when we stood cheek to cheek and looked at ourselves in the mirror, though, to tell the truth, I saw that her eyes shone more brightly than mine, as if they were lit up by the constant whirring of her mind.

Right out loud, Teresa mimicked the teacher, who pronounced the *p* in *Champs-Elysées*. Then she turned and stabbed me with a dazzling glance, while I felt envious and bewildered because just then I'd been feeling sorry for the teacher. Teresa's sassiness electrified me. And I was electrified by the way she pulled off her blue kneesocks in the school bathroom and flipped them into the air and then, with loving care, almost a caress, slipped on her fishnet stockings with the seam in back.

There were two things I couldn't stand: her way of pointing her nose in the air as if communing with who-knew-what lofty realm and then deigning to let her judgment descend. And there was the fact that she always liked the same boy I liked, so that if I said, "You know, I like so-and-so," she would invariably reply, "Actually, I like him too."

One afternoon—by now we were in middle school—we shut ourselves in her mother's bathroom to put on makeup, enough makeup so heads would turn. Then we went to take pictures of ourselves in a photo booth. The next day we gave the photo to a classmate whom we used as a go-between. We enclosed a note that asked, "Who of the two do you like more?" and ordered the boy to give everything to Marco, whom we were both crazy about. But this go-between was such a dolt that he delivered the answer to us in the middle of Latin class. The teacher, who was an old spinster, confiscated everything including our photo, sent the two of us to the principal's office, and put a black mark in the class roll. As soon as I set foot in the office, I felt a knot in my stomach, and the whole time the principal was giving me a lecture all I could think of was that "Jezebel" rhymes with "Go to hell." Teresa had dropped her great-lady act and was standing there with her head hanging down. The principal called our homes, but Teresa's parents were out and mine were away on a trip. That evening she and I phoned each other and, in the midst of tears, made a pact—we would both go to school the next day no matter what.

But Teresa didn't come—she left me to face the second part of the trial by myself. The principal stood up in front of the class and called me to the teacher's desk to shame me in front of all my classmates. I despised Teresa for not having come. But she did something even worse— another theft. This time she stole my best friend,

Anna—Anna who lived on the fifth floor of our apartment building.

One morning at school I see the two of them huddled together. They're giggling, having great fun together. When I go to join them, they barely say hello. I can tell they got together the day before, behind my back, and that my exile has just begun. That afternoon my stomachaches begin in earnest. I hardly sleep, with dreams that only add new pain or false hopes to my forlorn waking hours. This torment lasts an eternity. Then it abruptly comes to an end. One day I get on the elevator with Anna, and I get her back on my side. Without even saying hello, I start in. "Everybody says you like Paolo."

"Who, everybody?" she asks, alarmed.

"Oh, I don't know, Maddalena, Silvia . . . They told me that by now even Paolo knows."

Anna grows pale, and that's when I tell a lie, releasing the poisoned arrow. "They heard it from Teresa."

I know Anna very well, and I can see I've hit the target.

"It's not true that I like Paolo, it's not true at all. That's just some lie Teresa made up." And indeed, she says this with bitter resentment.

"Could be—who knows? Maybe it just

slipped out. I certainly haven't told anyone." I say this lightly, not wanting to put salt on her wound. I'm satisfied for now, but I'm savoring the revenge that's still to come. Because this is just the beginning. Teresa will pay. She'll pay for everything. She'll pay for all those things that I would like to do but don't dare.

judging

The road is white and the fields are yellow, speckled here and there with bloodred poppies. At night there are fireflies, hundreds, maybe thousands, but now it's daytime, and what I see are Gonda's black ears, bobbing up and down across the line between Earth and sky.

Papa and I are in the buggy on our way to the Cecchinis'—the tenant farmers at Civitella, my father's best farm. But first we'll stop in the town square, where we have an appointment with the farm manager.

Gonda's hooves echo in the main street. People look at us. They're curious and admiring, but they keep clear. A mother, misinterpreting Gonda's whinny, grabs the hand of her child— it's actually the horse's greeting—but the mare is too black, too alarming a creature. I can't help feeling a shiver of pride.

My father knows everybody, and people come up to him to say hello and compliment Gonda. Some of them pat her neck, which is shiny with sweat. There's also a brother of Papa's, Alfio, but they don't get along, they're still arguing over Grandfather's estate, even though he died years ago. Papa always pokes fun at Alfio, says that he's spiteful, greedy, and stingy, that he's not as handsome as Papa is, not as nice, and that's why no woman wanted to marry him.

And today too, after they greet each other, Papa starts poking at him: Is it true that Alfio's farm equipment was wrecked when the roof of the Montesca shed fell in because Alfio cut corners on repairs? Is it true that the farm at San Biagio will yield only a few tons because it rained too much? Strange—because on his own fields it rained just enough and now the wheat is waist high, shining, soft and golden. Is it true that at the club no one wants Alfio at the poker table because he always spoils the game, peeking at everyone's hand, whereas they've asked Papa to be president? Would Alfio like to see, here and now, which of the two of them can attract more people around him?

My father proposes that they each go to a corner of the square, and I'm to count how many people come up to talk with him and how many with Alfio.

"That's not fair," Alfio says. "You have the horse, of course you'll win."

"Fine. Then we'll have the girl and Gonda wait in the middle."

So there I am in the middle of the square halfway between Papa and my uncle with Gonda's bridle tight in my hands. I'm very anxious, partly because Gonda is restless and is making the wheels of the buggy clatter back and forth, and partly because I really want Papa to win, but I don't want Alfio's losing to be a total defeat. I see Alfio's thin little body, his nervous tic. On the other side of the square I see Papa's imposing figure. I see the gleam of Alfio's bald spot. On the other side I see Papa's full head of hair. And at that moment, even though I know I should be on Papa's side, I suffer for Alfio, so much that I want to shout, "Stop! That's enough—no game!" Gonda is becoming more impatient and starts pawing the pavement with her hoof. Meanwhile people are gathering around Papa, more and more of them, while a few nod to Alfio and walk on by.

By now it's useless for me to pay attention, useless for me to keep score. The only thing I can do is hang on to Gonda's bridle as she rears, lifting me into the air to celebrate Papa's triumph.

cousin mariapia

Before the September storms, there always came a Sunday afternoon when our vacation seemed too long, when Clara and I would be sitting in the cool front hall of the villa to escape the heavy air outside, paying attention to the relentless buzzing of a fly against the window-pane, an unmistakable sign of our boredom. One of us would lazily ask, "What'll we do now?" a bit irritated at seeing the other one in the same state of listlessness. We'd pretend to think about it for an instant. And then we'd give up with a sigh and end up sitting there, doing nothing for hours.

On afternoons like that, back home after a month at Versilia on the Tuscan coast, it would sometimes happen that some of my father's cousins would come for a visit. Mariapia was a widow, and she came with her old-maid sister, Elisabetta, and almost always with her eighteen-year-old daughter, Grazia. They came in their tiny sky blue car, the daughter at the wheel beside her enormous mother, who took up most of the space in front, and in the back, surprisingly skinny and swaying like a pendulum, was Elisabetta.

When we were all sitting around in wicker armchairs in front of the house, Grazia seemed quiet and wan, as if the imposing shadow of her mother darkened any gleam of adolescence in her.

But when the three of us, having left the grown-ups to their conversation, went for a walk in the park and Clara and I asked Grazia to tell us a story, she became a different person—she rattled on happily, and her whole face lit up.

Today she's telling us the story of *Wuthering Heights* and we're getting to the part where Heathcliff forces Cathy to marry his repulsive son, when Grazia stops and says, "If I show you something, do you swear you won't tell a soul?"

"What is it?" Clara says.

"First swear. Go on, make a cross with your fingers and kiss the cross."

My sister and I perform this ritual. Then, from the pocket of her flowered dress, Grazia takes out a photo.

"Look," she says with a little flutter of emotion, "this is the man I'm going to marry, my fiancé. Look how handsome he is, not a bit like Heathcliff's son. Look."

We look. A black-and-white photo. In the foreground there's a boy in a soldier's uniform. It looks like one of those photos of a dead person in a cemetery, with the background fading into white. We're at a loss for a moment. At last I manage to say in a thin voice, "He's cute." She doesn't notice and goes on with her story. "I kept seeing him in front of the repair shop where he works and he smiled at me, but I always looked away. But then one day I see him at the end of the street and when I go by he says, 'Hello, beautiful signorina,' and holds out a wonderful red rose. I look around to see if anyone's watching, then I take the rose and hide it under my coat and run away. Then I see him again at the same place, and this time we tell each other our names. And each time we meet we talk a little more, but if my mother's with me, we pretend not to know each other. I've gone with him in his car, up into the hills, and we kissed. Oh, I love him, I love him, I love him—but if my mother finds out she'll kill me, I have to think up excuses to go out, and I can't think of any more!"

I find this story more exciting than

Wuthering Heights. That night Clara and I discuss it.

"Here's what I think. I think he should kidnap her. They could find a priest to marry them in secret, and the two of us could be witnesses."

Clara says, "I don't think they'll get married."

"And why is that, excuse me very much."

"Because Mariapia doesn't want it."

"But you're not listening—I told you he'll kidnap her and they'll get married in secret."

"Yes, fine. But you'll see—when he comes to her house to kidnap her, Grazia will say no, that she doesn't have the courage to do it." Then, after a moment of silence, Clara adds, "Do you think Papa will be as terrible with us, the way Mariapia is with Grazia?"

"But what are you saying!" I blurt back. "Just because they're cousins doesn't mean they have to be alike."

But at the same time I have a sudden doubt because I remember the way Papa says that if any suitors show up for us he'll kick their backsides.

Not long after that, Mariapia, Elisabetta, and Grazia came to visit. Grazia had swollen eyes. I couldn't wait for the grown-ups to settle into their chairs in front of the house so we could go to the park. Once she was alone with us, Grazia said that it was all over, that her mother had begun to suspect and one day she'd followed her to the gas station where they'd agreed to meet to go up into the hills, that her mother had dragged her home, hitting her the whole way, and that Aunt Elisabetta had had the husband of a friend of hers telephone the owner of the shop so that the boy was fired. Now she could only leave the house if she went with her mother, and next year her mother was sending her away to boarding school. She burst into tears, and Clara and I each held one of her hands. Then, still sobbing, she said, "My mother says he's lower class and for me to get it into my head that I'll marry at least a notary." She burst into tears again, and I tried to find something comforting to say, and I racked my brains for some ray of hope or some dramatic turn, but nothing came to mind so I began to cry too, praying with all my might that Papa wouldn't take after his cousin Mariapia.

the crossing

This ship is a city without danger where Clara and I can live on our own. Of course our parents are there, but we don't have to ask their permission and there's so much space we don't have territorial disputes with our brothers. We have a cabin all to ourselves—the key is by turns a hard little bulge in my pocket or my sister's.

We can do whatever we want whenever we please—either play "sky" on the promenade deck or go to the movies—in the morning, for free. When we come out we're blinded by the unbroken light of the sky and the sea. Some nights, with blankets pulled up to our noses, we lie on deck and count the stars, starting all over again when we lose count until we begin to see red and green planets and it's time to go to bed. For the first time in our lives we stay up till dawn, but it turns out to be a disappointing paleness.

One morning we see a whale's spout draw a mustache on the horizon, but no one believes us, neither our parents nor our brothers, four sniggering faces at the dinner table. We ignore them—we're strong after all these days that are ours alone.

The crossing to America lasted ten days, and then my mother pointed to the Statue of Liberty and the ship came into port, entering her slip to a volley of skyrockets. In the crowd on the pier there are Mama's cousins, their eyes glistening and laughing, their mouths forming words that are lost in the general cheering and fanfare.

In New York, Mama spends all her time talking with her cousins, so Clara and I always go out with Papa, walking for hours along avenues that are like immense diving boards stretching out into space. For some reason I kept expecting to see Cary Grant coming out of a revolving door from one of the buildings in Midtown, his necktie blowing in the wind—all of it in black and white.

Papa took Clara and me to a huge store

with three floors where there was nothing but toys.

At the entrance he turned us loose, saying, "You can pick three toys each." He turned to me and said, "You keep an eye on the clock. When the hands reach here and here it will be half past ten, and we'll meet at the cash register. All right?" Yes, that's fine, but I'm already losing my head and I say to Clara that we'll never manage to choose, all those possibilities are making my head spin. And of course I go wrong. In the coloring section alone there are two dozen shelves. I finally pick a box of crayons, which I don't usually like to use, but on the box there's a tiger with three tiger cubs, my favorite animal of the moment. Then I grab a teddy bear dressed like a forest ranger, not much of anything but certainly better than my next choice, completely absurd— a baseball mitt, for a sport that it has never entered my head to play but whose red stitching and beautiful leathery toughness somehow hypnotize me.

When I meet my father at the cashier's counter I'm discontented and upset, as if I've been defeated in a way I can't bear to admit, and I start complaining about how cold I am because of the air-conditioning. So it all ends badly with me getting a scolding: "Stop that sniveling. What a whiner you are! And you're spoiled."

We take a trip to the north in a rented station wagon that for days and days I saw as completely immense until my eyes got used to that big country, filled with highways that had no curves. We reached Cape Cod on a gray afternoon, with the sea, the sky, and the dunes all the same color. My brothers and I suddenly got a desperate urge to run on the beach, so we began chanting our "chorus of persuasion" that consisted of each of us, one after the other, saying "Come *on,* Papa!" faster and faster. It worked. We spilled out of the car and ran headlong toward the dunes. They were so high that as I watched my brothers scramble farther and farther up they became smaller and smaller, and when they reached the crest they were as small as shriveled trees on a gigantic mountain and I was afraid that a gust of wind would blow them away. I yelled with relief when I saw them come tumbling down to me in billows of sand.

We rented a bungalow by the sea, and for the first time Clara and I were separated, each of us sharing a bedroom with a brother, she with Carlo and I with Pietro. That evening, as we lay in our beds, Pietro taught me the game of composing the ideal menu. I always put in lobster, which I'd discovered on Cape Cod. We ate them at rough wooden tables with long plastic bibs tied around our necks. I would say, "I want another," and Mama would say no and Papa would say yes. She thought it would make me sick, but Papa was happy that I liked something that much.

The people we met were certainly nicer than in France, where, whatever you asked them, they answered with an irritated shrug or a puff of disdain. But in contrast to Italians, each nice in his own way, the Americans had a ready-made niceness—set formulas that were always telling you to do something. The gas station attendant said, "Have a nice day." The waiter said, "Enjoy your meal." The bellboy said, "Watch your step" as he showed us into our hotel room.

One time when Papa was in a terrible mood because we had a flat tire and it was getting dark, Mama laughed and said, "Don't worry! Be happy!" and he started laughing too.

After Cape Cod we went to see Niagara Falls, but I found it depressing. The incessant roaring in the middle of all that mist upset me, and at the museum they showed us a barrel in which an old woman had thrown herself over the falls and died. That evening, however, we slept in a motel, all of us in the same room, and we took turns telling jokes in the dark, and when I closed my eyes I hoped it was forever, now that I was there, once more happy and safe.

the march sisters

For a long time, every afternoon around three, there was a quarter of an hour of traffic in our building between the first floor and the fifth. Clara and I, along with Anna and Gabriella, loaded the elevator with dresses, purses, scarves, hats, umbrellas, a rocking chair, a trunk—and then a teapot, teacups, and books—and we kept it going up and down, up and down, while the residents of the other floors looked at us sternly. It would have been useless to explain what on earth we were up to or how important it was, because they wouldn't have understood in the least. At that very moment they were no longer Monsieur Gramont or Madame Desmoulins with children and grandchildren of their own, but citizens of the building—co-owners whose right to the undisturbed and prompt use of the elevator (clearly posted in the regulations) was being intolerably violated. So, pretending not to hear the pounding on the elevator doors and avoiding the icy looks of those who'd given up and were using the stairs, we lowered our heads and carried on with our work.

Depending on whether it was a Monday or one of the other weekdays, we were moving the stage setting of our favorite game, Little Women, either from our friends' apartment to ours or from ours to theirs. Since certain indispensable elements belonged either to them or to us—too bad for the neighbors. It was a case of absolute necessity.

The first time we played Little Women we had to assign the parts, and I was in a panic because I knew exactly which part I wanted but was not at all sure of getting.

Anna, the eldest, will be Margaret, called Meg, the oldest March sister. Sensible and poised, she'll wear the long, blue, somewhat severe dress that belonged to Anna's grandmother, and she'll wear her hair in a long braid. So far, so good, we all agree. But now my anxiety has increased because if we keep on assigning the parts by age, it's all over for me. And in fact I hear

Anna saying to me, "You're a year younger than me, so you'll be Jo, the second—"

"No, that's impossible, that's out!" I suddenly explode, stamping my feet because I want, I want no matter what, the part of sweet, tender, beloved Beth, who plays the piano and then comes down with scarlet fever and dies, breaking everybody's heart.

"Well, who do you want to be then if you won't be Jo?" Anna asks.

"Beth" comes out in a hoarse whisper, but when they all ask why, I can't say—I'm in the grip of a shameful dark wish, and the more ashamed I am, the more I insist. "I want to be Beth." I'm so unreasonable and obstinate, even threatening to go home, that Anna is forced to give in. "All right," she says, "but that means that Gabriella will have to be Jo."

It's only now, now that I'm worn out and guilty, that I can think of plausible arguments. "Yes—Gabriella is perfect for the part. She's independent and lively, just like Jo. And she likes books, just like Jo. Isn't that right, Gabriella? Whereas I prefer music. . . ."

So Clara will be Amy. They're both the youngest, and they both have turned-up noses.

My sister protests, "But I'm not vain like

Amy." She says this in a whiny voice, on the brink of a tantrum, and I'm so afraid that something will happen to unsettle the casting that I sweetly reassure her, "Of course you're not. When you act you have to pretend to be a certain way, and you're not vain at all, so if you can make us all *believe* you are, you'll be a really good actress. See?"

Yes, she seems to have gotten the idea, because she's rummaging through the basket of barrettes, ribbons, and brooches, reconciled to adorning her hair as elaborately as the script calls for. "And don't forget this," I say, handing her a clothespin. "You have to put it on your nose the way Amy does to keep it from growing too wide."

"But it'll hurt."

"If you want to be a good actress, you have to be prepared to make sacrifices," I say sharply, I the good Beth. Anna comes to the rescue. "You don't have to wear it the whole time. I'll give you a signal during the scene when it's time to put it on." And each of us finishes gathering up the bits and pieces of her costume in silence.

I consider my booty on a corner of the bed: a long satin dress with a purple skirt and a lilac top, a snood, a bowl of flour, and gray eye shadow.

I get dressed in front of the mirror and gather my hair up in the snood. With a cotton ball I cover my face with flour, a nice thick layer. With the eye shadow I turn my eyes into two ghostly sockets. I'm very happy with the effect, and I ignore Clara when she says that I look as if I'm already dead. Anna and Gabriella don't seem particularly keen either, but because of my earlier outburst they avoid saying anything. At last we're ready, and Anna says, "I'll begin with the scene where the sisters get the letter from their father after he's gone to war."

I object, "But that's practically at the beginning. If we do all the chapters we'll never get to the end."

"Well, I'm sorry, but what's the big hurry?" Anna asks, beginning to lose patience.

"It's not that we have to hurry," I try to explain. "It's just that the story gets more beautiful toward the middle." But this time she has no intention of giving up. The play will go on according to the novel. So we do the scene with the letter, the scene where they meet the kind Laurie (played by an eight-inch wooden Pinocchio), who's the nephew of the grumpy and very rich Mister Lawrence, who gives a piano to Beth (we also play that scene), et cetera et cetera. Then—finally—we get to my big moment.

So far I've played my part wearing a mask of flour; now I dump the whole bowl onto my face. With the eye shadow I transform my eyes into even more livid slits, and as a final touch I put some gray eye shadow on my lips. And I'm ready to die, body and soul. When I lie down on the bed, I actually feel ill. A moment later, surrounded by the loving care of my sisters, I'm about to faint, and when I pronounce my last words of comfort to each of them, tears well up in my half-closed eyes. When I hear them whispering their lament for the angel of goodness, loyalty, and generosity that I have always been, I see my wingéd soul fly up to Paradise in a triumph of silver clouds. At the very end, when Meg shuts my eyes, tears of joy flood my face. I lie there sweetly drowning as wet lumps of flour cascade onto the pillow.

rue du bac

We're in the car—Mama and Clara in front, I in the back. It's three in the afternoon, a cold rain. The smell of the plastic on the seats is making me a little sick. We're going to Madame Petruchskaya's dance class in the Rue du Bac, and my hands, which are resting on the seat, are trembling.

Today is not a class like the others.

Today Madame Petruchskaya will pick the most gifted girls and nominate them for the ballet school of the Opera.

Clara is looking out the window and is telling the story, to no one in particular, of the lady who came to her classroom that morning, and her eyes were painted all around with blue and when the principal said, "Children, this is your substitute teacher, Miss Azzurra," Clara burst out laughing and her friend Benedetta too, but luckily the substitute teacher didn't notice and neither did the principal.

And now Clara laughs all over again, merrily.

"Lucky her," I think.

I also think that if Mama runs into the car in front of us, maybe we'll be late.

And then I think that I'll say I'm feeling sick. But I don't say anything and stay quiet the whole car ride.

There's not much traffic, and all too soon Mama lets us off in front of the building (parents aren't admitted during the audition). She calls out, "Good luck, children!" Clara looks at me, happy to have a chance to say, *"Merde."* A minute later we're in the front hall in front of the beautiful staircase that leads up to the salle de danse. I go up behind my sister, taking slow steps, staring at the raindrops that are running off my raincoat and falling on the red carpet, making a *petits-pois* design.

In the changing room there's the usual stink of sweat. I take off my dress, and I'm cold. Even my black tights are cold. I put on my black leotard and pink ballet slippers. I'm the last one.

Clara tells me to hurry up, the others are already in the salle de danse.

The salle is immense, with big mirrors and barres along the wall. The parquet floor is brightly polished. In the corner there's Madame Rostand, seated at the piano.

With her dyed platinum blond hair, a long skirt and black leotard, and her long staff with the silver knob, Madame Petruchskaya is in the middle of her instructions, her Russian *r* more pronounced than usual. She explains what the test will consist of (which steps, figures, and so on) and what she expects from us (posture, the spirit of the dance). While she's talking I picture Alba, Mama's ballerina cousin, the star of the New York City Ballet. I see the photo of her divine arabesque under the spotlights and what Madame Petruchskaya is saying gets confused with what Alba told me: "The dance, darling, is a sublime and damnable cocktail of blood, sweat, and tears."

There are ten of us girls from age seven to eleven, arranged by height. I'm the tallest, so I'm the last. In front of me is Natasha, who isn't Russian, however. She's French and very unpleasant. She's already drawing herself completely erect, but her arms are like soft parentheses along her body with her curled fingers just brushing her legs. I'm hypnotized by her perfect figure and posture and totally neglect my own. Now it's her turn and she starts with her chin held high, which gives an arch to her back and a direction to her steps. Her feet touch the pavement, then fly off it with the ease and assurance of someone who's going into and coming out of her own house. At the end there's applause.

Now it's my turn. But my eyes are fixed on my shoes, on the curved line they trace on my feet, on the ugly contrast between that pink and the black of the tights. I barely hear the piano and I move as if I'm in a dream, the whole while absorbed by that pink line.

I don't advance to the auditions for the Opera School, nor does Clara. Madame Petruchskaya communicates this to my mother and then declaims, "What can one say, *chère madame*? The dance is a religion. To have faith in oneself and faith in the dance is a gift from Heaven, a blessing. . . ."

In the car on our way home, Mama repeats this line, mimicking Madame Petruchskaya's Russian *r*s. Then she says conclusively, "What a fanatic that woman is." While Clara is laughing, I sink into a gloomy meditation on this last of a series of proofs of my resistance to divine grace.

peregrinations

I was in upper middle school when she joined our class—the only girl taller than I. She had a far-off, ethereal look, and when she sat down at the desk next to mine a cascade of golden hair swirled around her, a veil through which I caught a glimpse of mysterious other worlds. There was something old-fashioned or perhaps timeless about her clothes, like the eternal robes of angels—and also something threadbare, faded, and completely indifferent to the rules of girlish elegance to which my own outfit of *jeune fille de bonne famille* conformed.

We took to walking part of the way home together. By a strange coincidence, Eleonora lived in the very same apartment that had been ours when we had first come to Paris—the apartment with the little garden where years earlier Ruga, my pet turtle, had been lost. When I told her how I'd looked and looked for Ruga, she told me that when she was little her father had given her a mongoose, Syria, who had disappeared. Eleonora had cried a lot, until one day, when she was standing mournfully in her garden, a bird landed at her feet. And how amazed she'd been to see that around its neck the bird was wearing Syria's collar. Then she said the name aloud and the bird answered her with a warble. "The souls of living things don't die when their bodies die," she explained. "They pass on into the bodies of other beings, even into plants. So if you keep looking—really looking—you'll find your Ruga."

I was very impressed and immediately set to work. But since I didn't know exactly what distinctive sign would guide me, I settled on the easiest: the shell. For days and days my investigation failed to come up with a single man, flower, or animal endowed with anything resembling natural armor. I confessed to Eleonora that I was discouraged.

"Don't worry," she said, consoling me. "We'll look for Ruga together with the pendulum."

We're at her house, seated at the dining room table. Spread in rows in front of us is a child's set of geography cards. Eleonora is kneeling on a chair, casually holding the pendulum, while I feel as if I'm about to enter the Sybil's cave. "The pendulum will tell us what kind of living thing your turtle has changed into." She tells me, "Close your eyes and concentrate on her name. You have to see it in your mind, written in capital letters, like a big shining sign."

I have faith in her, and I do what she says, and before long I see enormous letters on my closed eyelids, tongues of flame that hurt my eyes.

"There," Eleonora says. "On that card— the woman scything—the pendulum's swinging from right to left. That means that Ruga's soul isn't in a woman. You go on concentrating—I'll try the tiger card."

We try a number of them—the rose, the alpinist, the forest, the mountain—yes, even the mountain because apparently it happens that souls can take refuge in rocks. But the pendulum persists in its cycle of denial. I'm beginning to think that maybe Ruga isn't dead at all, that she's off somewhere leading the life of an old turtle. But then the pendulum starts swinging the other way on the card of the Japanese woman.

"Excuse me, but you just said that it wasn't a woman," I say, puzzled and a bit annoyed.

Eleanora once again reassures me, saying that at times it's necessary to interpret the answers of the pendulum and that maybe her father will be able to help us.

The father, who seems to me quite old, is a marquis and a Buddhist. He has a silver mustache whose tapered ends point straight up, like little missiles. Without hesitating he answers our question. "If the pendulum reacted positively to the card of the Japanese woman, it means that the turtle was reincarnated not in France but in the Orient . . . perhaps in Japan, or perhaps in China, in India, in Indochina, in the Philippines, in Indonesia. . . ." But I'm not listening to him anymore, and my head is spinning at the thought of all the peregrinations I'll have to undertake to find my Ruga. I'm disappointed, frustrated by my own frustration, and when Eleanora and I leave her father, I start crying with rage. She strokes my hand and says, "But if you love Ruga so much, why don't you try to let her go, why not be happy that she's alive even if she's gone away to lead her own life? Why does she have to be tied to you?"

"That's easy for you to say," I snap. I feel

hurt and mean. "You're not normal, you live on air, you're not attached to anything or anyone. You don't even have a ring or a pen or a dress that you really care about."

That time Eleonora said nothing, but I saw a shadow cross her usually serene face and I felt terrible. The next day I gave her my shocking pink felt-tip pen.

Then, having abandoned the turtle to her exotic avatar, we threw ourselves into a new series of experiments. We used the pendulum to help us with the subject of our Italian composition; to discover the mysterious identity of Belphagor, the phantom of the Louvre; to tell us where the kidnappers were hiding little René from Lyon. Next we tried telepathy—we sent a single letter to each other, then a color, a word, a thought—putting the communion of our minds to harder and harder tests.

Together we summoned strange impish spirits who pinched my behind and a bookseller by the name of Erasmus who had been burned at the stake in Bruges in the sixteenth century, whose mournful soul communicated with me by rapping three times on the table. I forgot my other friends, Anna and Teresa, and our obsession with dresses, hair bands, and shoes, and the hours we'd spent lying side by side on a bed pulling out split ends and examining with biblical exegeses the ambiguities in a sentence spoken by some boy we liked.

I'd gone through the looking glass, into that country where she had come to be called Eleonora (her real name was actually Diana), and her brothers (named Tancredi and Federico) answered to the names of Brando and Manfredo. Her father—right in front of us—read a magazine, *Il Borghese,* with photos of nude women. From time to time, wrapped in his London Fog raincoat and always a few steps ahead of us, he took us to the Theosophical Society, where they played a music I'd never heard while the listeners swayed their heads keeping time to the arcane repetitive rhythm. Sometimes I felt like laughing, but only because I didn't feel worthy of all that mystery.

Eleonora and I are drawing a comic strip—the adventures of a mad orchestra conductor and a worm who plays first violin. But just as we reach the third episode Eleonora announces that her father has run out of money and the whole family is going back to Italy before the end of the year. I cry. I'm in despair. I ask to see Eleonora's father. He receives me.

Still crying, I beg him not to take Eleonora away from me. "Without her I can't live, can't you see? She's everything to me, she's like Clara, a sister—even more—she's practically my twin."

He listens to me intently, raising an eyebrow. Then he tells me a long complicated story about two mermaids who are friends, about how they lose each other and find each other again and again during their voyage from a small sea to the vast ocean—and I can tell that I'm not going to get anywhere with him.

Then I try my father. I ask him for a loan for Eleonora's father. He tells me that things like that aren't done, that they end up offending people, and that anyway it's not so much that Eleonora's father has run out of money but that he likes living in a certain way—now here, now there—and that we have to respect the way other people are.

"Fine," I blurt out. "I see. It's the same story over and over. I lose my animals, I lose my friends, I lose everything, and somehow I'm supposed to go on being happy."

champ de mars

We're walking on top of a sea of cars like Jesus on water. My father's holding our hands, and Clara and I climb up and down hoods and roofs, out of breath from excitement, taking care not to slip if someone tries to bar the way.

The sidewalks are thick with people who overflow onto the street and try to make their way between the stopped cars, but there's no room, so a few people—and then more and more—join us on that makeshift route.

It is a hot evening in May. May 1968 in Paris.

The demonstration on the Champ de Mars spills over into the streets that surround the park. Along with the hysteria of automobile horns, there are slogans, songs, shouts, all in a festival atmo-

sphere that at times overheats and explodes—
a shop window breaks into pieces, there's an
exchange of insults and shoving, a brawl. I cling to
Papa's hand, my buoy in the stormy sea. I'm
sweating from the effort of keeping my footing on
the high, slippery terrain, on this car roof on which
there are now four of us. And now the furious
driver gets out of the car and yells at us to get off,
get off the roof of his car right away, we're nothing
but good-for-nothing vandals. His eyes are blood-
shot bulbs just at the height of my feet, and there
he is grabbing at my calf. I have a new kind of fear,
one I've never felt, strangely pleasant, a light current that runs along the wiring of my skin—since
my father is with me, nothing, nothing serious or
nasty or irreparable can happen, not even now
that the driver's hand is on my leg and pulling,
pulling at me to make me get down, to make me
fall, while my father is pulling me the other way
shouting at him not to touch me, to wait a minute
and we'll get down on our own. The hand lets go,
and I end up bumping into my father and I laugh.
But in his eyes there's a shadow, the first ripple of
worry, very likely because my mother didn't want
him to take us to see the demonstration.

He helps us get down from the roof, and
somehow we make our way to the sidewalk. Then,

walled in by the crowd, our faces jammed against a sweater or a plaid shirt in front of us, we're swept along toward the Champ de Mars.

I don't recognize the open space where Clara and I play every day, I can't find it: the park has become a single living thing, a body that's breathing and pushing toward a platform that's been set up in the middle. On it someone is speaking and the crowd is still pushing, listening with its thousands of ears to that voice ringing from the loudspeaker.

I'm squeezed into the middle of the crowd, shivering each time it responds to the voice either with applause or with a cyclopean roar. But I can't see, I can't see a thing, not even the lady on the stage whom I want to see so badly.

I ask my father to put me up on his shoulders. From up there I see her. She's dressed like Mama in a midlength skirt, a cardigan, and a necklace that seems to be a string of pearls.

"Who is she, Papa, that lady who's talking?"

"Simone de Beauvoir. A writer, a philosopher."

"And what's she saying?" I keep at him because I don't understand a single word or, to tell the truth, the whole situation.

He says, "It would take too long, I'll tell you when we get home," and he hushes me.

So at home I try again.

"She was telling all those kids that it's fine to protest for freedom and justice, it's good to do that, but everyone has to take responsibility for his own life, take charge of his own life and basically be himself."

"Have you done all those things?" I ask, hoping that a concrete example will make it all clear to me.

"Ah . . . I'm not sure. Yes, probably yes . . . At any rate I've never felt that I was living someone else's life." My father answers me in such a vague, pensive voice that I'm left more than ever in the dark.

persephone

I'm skating on an ice rink that I've been on before. I go around a few times confidently, not hurrying, proud of how well I'm doing, how good my balance is. But then I feel something like a breath on the back of my neck—another breath and then another and then the heavy breathing of a whole crowd behind me. I know who they are, and I don't turn around. I pick up the pace, but imperceptibly, so they won't know I'm scared. But then I realize that it's not me making myself go faster, it's their breath that's pushing me. Every lap is faster and faster, and I feel my skate blades vibrating on the ice, they're about to break or else melt the ice—I know this—and I lose control, I'm going to smash into the railing and the telephone rings and I wake up.

From her room I hear my mother ask, "Is he dead?"

I sit on my bed gasping, trying not to know what I know, but all the lights in the house are on in the middle of the night, my brothers are awake, and Clara is awake beside me and it's the end, what I know has become true.

My father went out at eight to take his new sports car for a test run with a friend.

The parents of our friends come down from the fifth floor in their pajamas. Mama is crying, the mother of our friends is crying, and Clara is holding my hand. The father of our friends goes up to his apartment and comes back down with his overcoat on.

My mother is sitting on the little sofa in the front hall, I'm standing in front of her, my knees against hers, my hands in hers. She swallows once and then again and says to me, "I'm going to the hospital now with your brothers. Papa is there, there's still a thread of hope." With her look she's imploring me to believe, if I believe then she can too, but in my eyes she sees my father's heavy body hanging by a thread and she begins to sob again.

Clara and I stay at home, along with the

mother of our friends. She comes with us into our bedroom, lets us push our beds together, and sits beside us as we lie down. I promise God that if he saves my father I'll become a nun, but it's a half-hearted vow because I don't believe in that sort of bartering and because I don't really want to become a nun, and then I'm overcome with a fear of God, of a God who demands these things, and I hate him and I hate myself, a Judas traitor. I sit up because I'm having trouble breathing, but there's the hand of our friend that presses me down and stays on my chest as she says, "That's a good girl, sleep. Try to sleep." Time stays still, broken only by a wave that every so often swells and crests inside me and then breaks and roars in my ears, leaving me stunned and deafened.

At last they come back. Papa is dead. Outside it's dawn, but the city is extinguished. A crowd of people arrives, a swarm of whispers and sobs. Some bankers come. They wish to offer their condolences and to make sure that the widow will honor the debts of the deceased. Some of my father's friends take my brothers aside, remind them of their new responsibilities. No one says anything to my sister and me, and there are so many people around Mama that we can't get close to her. Maybe she's forgotten about us. Holding hands, we drift invisibly through the rooms, but each of us is alone—a new strange sheet of glass separates us. We go up to one group and then another, and perhaps someone gives us a gentle pat. A friend of Pietro's arrives, he's someone I like, and I come out of my daze, proud of my tragedy, for the first time worthy of his attention, but he gives me a hurried kiss and goes off to find my brother. Then Dame Dame comes, and it's as if we've found our bodies again. She washes our hands and faces and dresses us, she herself is crying the whole time. She closes the door to our bedroom, makes us sit down on the bed, and talks about Papa and how we must pray for his soul. And then I see it, I see it taking off, headed straight for Paradise, my prayers and Clara's are the motors. Then I see it change as it's flying, change into a huge butterfly, velvet brown and violet, or into a golden eagle— and I watch it for a moment without reaching out to hold it back, it's happy to be free in the way Eleonora explained to me. But then right after that I see Persephone, taken from the world of the living, dragged down into the world of the dead, but her mother arranged that she could come back to spend a little time with her, and then my eyes close and I give in to the darkness. Finally I begin to cry, and in between sobs I say in a whisper, "Oh, Papa, wherever it is you're going, don't forget me."

A NOTE ABOUT THE AUTHOR

Linda Ferri was born in Rome in 1957. She coauthored with Nanni Moretti the screenplay *The Son's Room,* which won the Palme d'Or at the 2001 Cannes Film Festival and was released by Miramax in 2002. This is her first novel.

A NOTE ABOUT THE TRANSLATOR

John Casey is the author of *Spartina,* winner of the 1989 National Book Award for fiction, *The Half-Life of Happiness, Supper at the Black Pearl, An American Romance,* and *Testimony and Demeanor.* He is a professor of English Literature at the University of Virginia. He has translated *You're an Animal, Viskovitz!* by Alessandro Boffa.

A NOTE ON THE TYPE

This book was set in De Vinne, an American typeface that is actually a recutting by Gustav Schroeder of French Elzevir. It was introduced by the Central Type Foundry of St. Louis in 1889. Named in honor of Theodore Low De Vinne, whose nine-story plant, called the Fortress, was the first building in New York City erected expressly for printing, the type has a delicate quality obtained by the contrast between the thick and thin parts of letters. An enormously popular type during the early part of this century, De Vinne combines easy readability with a nostalgic feeling.

Composed by Creative Graphics
Allentown, Pennsylvania

Printed and bound by Berryville Graphics
Berryville, Virginia

Book design by Pamela G. Parker